MURDER APPLIED FOR

Borgo Press Books by LLOYD BIGGLE, JR.

All the Colors of Darkness (Jan Darzek)
The Chronicide Mission
The Fury Out of Time
A Galaxy of Strangers
The Light That Never Was
Monument
Murder Applied For: A Classic Crime Mystery (with Kenneth Lloyd Biggle)
Murder Jambalaya: A J. Pletcher & Raina Lambert Mystery
The Rule of the Door and Other Fanciful Regulations
Silence Is Deadly (Jan Darzek)
The Still, Small Voice of Trumpets (Cultural Survey)
This Darkening Universe (Jan Darzek)
Watchers of the Dark (Jan Darzek)
The Whirligig of Time (Jan Darzek)
The World Menders (Cultural Survey)
The World That Death Made: A Science Fiction Novel (with Kenneth Lloyd Biggle)

MURDER APPLIED FOR

A CLASSIC CRIME MYSTERY

LLOYD BIGGLE, JR.

& KENNETH LLOYD BIGGLE

THE BORGO PRESS

MMXIII

MURDER APPLIED FOR

FIRST EDITION

Published by Wildside Press LLC

www.wildsidebooks.com

DEDICATION

With Special Thanks to Donna
Biggle Emerson, My Sister and Editor

CONTENTS

INTRODUCTION

My father, Lloyd Biggle, Jr., died in 2002 after a long battle with leukemia.

He left behind a legacy in the written word of science fiction, and mystery novels, short stories, and novellas. He also left behind about every letter, note, story idea, and outline that he ever possessed, a lot of it very neatly cataloged, stored and boxed, and some just…well…boxed.

It is now the year 2013. My sister and I are still making our way through this lifetime of material.

This story, found in one of the manuscript boxes has a date of: "8/30/64." The manuscript had revision pages that were not added to the original manuscript. This makes me believe that the final form was never submitted to a publisher. I have added them where possible to make the final version complete.

Murder Applied For is unusual as it involves an insurance investigator, and a lot of insurance practices that were probably the norm in the early 1960s. My father *was* an insurance agent before and into the beginning of his writing career, giving him this knowledge base.

This is an early Biggle story, and reflects his developing style of writing, which did change throughout his lifetime.

I hope that you find this story and character concept to be enjoyable.

—Kenneth Lloyd Biggle

CHAPTER ONE

The patrol car swerved, came to a halt, and Ron Webber opened his eyes and looked about dazedly. He hadn't thought to ask where they were going, and now he found himself blinking in surprise at the arrow and the flickering neon words: "Ambulance Entrance."

He said, "Where are we?"

"Municipal Hospital," the young officer said.

Webber nodded, opened a rear door, and climbed out. It had to be a hospital, he supposed. Either that, or a funeral parlor, because Carter City didn't have a morgue. There was even a highly unfunny comic song about that:

"It has doctors by the dozens, it has chiropractors, too
And hospitals and pharmacies and nursing homes galore;
You can get your body sutured, any hour, day or night
But you can't die, 'cause it hasn't got a morgue."

Webber took two steps, turned, and waited numbly. The two officers were talking in guarded tones, and their sudden laughter jolted him. He scowled resentfully, thrust his hands into his pockets, and rocked back and forth on his heels, shivering in the warm, humid night air.

The young officer got out, carelessly slammed both doors, and moved on ahead of him. He turned, holding the door open for Webber, and Webber set his feet in motion and entered the air conditioned corridor of the hospital.

The officer caught up with him, and their footsteps clicked in a confused pattern on the tiled floor. He touched Webber's arm, opened a door, and a white-coated attendant stepped forward to meet them.

"Sure was a hot day," the officer said. "It almost feels cold in here."

Webber made no response. He wanted no casual conversation in that chill, sterile room. He wanted only to do his duty and depart. In the presence of the crushed body of a friend, the death-room was a suffocating place.

The ceremony was brief—a gesture, a mechanical gesture to the letter of the law. The sheet was raised, and Webber glanced and nodded. "It's him. It's Frank Milford."

The officer shrugged. "Tough," he said.

Webber thought bitterly, "It's all in a day's work for him." And then, because he knew that was the way it had to be, he wondered why he was bitter.

The officer paused for a whispered conversation with an attendant, and Webber turned away. He needed some time to himself, some time to think. There would be relatives to notify, if Frank had any. He couldn't recall. There would be funeral arrangements to make, and Frank's personal effects to look after, and probably other things. And there was Gloria. Someone—anyone, so long as it was not Ron Webber—would have to tell Gloria.

He moved out into the corridor, walking quickly.

He heard a shuffle of footsteps as the officer hurried to catch up with him. Just then the outside door banged, and the second officer strode toward them. He muttered something into the ear of Webber's escort. The escort nodded, and turned politely to Webber.

"If you don't mind, Mr. Webber, we'd like to have you...."

Back up the corridor they went and this time it was a girl. Webber looked quickly and turned away, carrying with him a grim impression of blonde hair and a small, serious face. The eyes would be blue, he thought, and she wouldn't be beautiful, but she'd be nice-looking and probably have the kind of figure that gets spontaneous whistles on street corners. He wondered if some young man would be heart-broken about this.

"No," he said. "I don't recognize her."

Again they walked way. The officer got in step with Webber, and their footsteps clicked rhythmically. Webber glanced sideways at him.

"Was it the same accident? Was she with Frank?"

"It was a different accident."

His bland expression told Webber nothing. Webber shrugged, and kept to himself the moral outrage he felt at the calloused manner in which the police exhibited dead bodies.

They stepped through the door, and the faintly-stirring, warm night air instantly engulfed them. From the main thoroughfare at the end of the ambulance drive came sputtering traffic noises and the flash of neon signs. Webber shook his head confusedly. What had he been thinking about? Relatives, if any. And funeral arrangements. And he'd have to track down things like bank accounts and bonds and insurance policies. And someone would have to tell Gloria.

The officer opened the rear door for him.

"Many thanks," Webber said. "But I can find my way home all right. I'd just as soon be alone, if you don't mind."

The officer nodded. If an expressionless face could possibly be called sympathetic, his was. "The Old Man wants to talk to you," he said.

"Sure. First thing in the morning, all right?"

The answer was polite, but unmistakably firm. "He'd like to talk with you now."

At the office of the Chief of Police Webber dismissed his escort with a nod, opened the door himself, and firmly closed it behind him. He moved boldly across the room, shattered the silence by kicking a chair into position in front of the desk, and sat down.

"Well?" he said.

There were two men in the office. The one behind the desk squared his shoulders, and rasped, "Took you long enough." The booming voice seemed much too large for the small room.

"Those nursemaids you gave me were doing the driving," Webber said. "They managed a nice reckless twenty. They're almost as daring behind a wheel as you are."

The Chief leaned forward, elbows on his desk, and glared. His cigar quivered at a jaunty angle. A scar line on his right cheek stood out sharply in the white glare of the overhead lamp. That, and the two missing fingers on his left hand were mementos of occasions when he'd saved Carter City the expense of a trial by presenting it with an outlaw duly certified guilty and dead.

Big, robust, tough-looking, he'd graduated from the school of hard knocks with honors of his own making. Only the touch of grey in his hair suggested that he was old enough to be Webber's father—which he was.

He was Ronald Webber, Senior, and his fondest hope in life had been that his only son would choose a police career. But Webber had stopped growing at three inches below the minimum height of five feet eight for which the Old Man had never quite forgiven him. They'd had a parting of the ways when Webber finished college, and their rare meetings since then had been less than affectionate.

The other man in the room was Detective-Lieutenant Robert Hendricks, who specialized in homicide when Carter City had any. He occupied a chair at one end of the desk. He was slumped back with his long legs stretched out at an uncomfortable angle, and his gaunt face wore a look of indescribable weariness.

A briefcase lay on the desk in front of them. The gilt was gone from the lettering, but the name was still legible. *Frank Milford.*

Hendricks gave Webber a belated nod of recognition, and smiled faintly. The Old Man continued to glare. Webber waited for the best part of a minute before he edged forward impatiently.

"All right," he said. "I'm not on the police force. I have to work tomorrow. What's the problem?"

The Old Man's face reddened slightly beneath his tan. He kept his teeth clamped on the cigar and his eyes on Webber. He muttered sideways to Hendricks, "You take it."

Hendricks leaned forward and spoke softly. "Frank was an old friend of mine, Ron. Have you known him long?"

"Since I went to work for National Credit. Four years next month."

"And you've shared an apartment with him—how long?"

Webber thought for a moment. "Seventeen months."

"Did Frank have any enemies?"

Webber straightened up slowly. Hendricks had slumped back in his chair again, apparently relaxed, but his hands were tense, his fingers tapping soundlessly on the desk. His gaze was fixed on the opposite wall. The Old Man kept his eyes on Webber.

"I thought it was an accident," Webber said.

"It's on the books as a hit-and-run accident. Did he have any enemies?"

"Not that I know of."

Hendricks got to his feet absently. Five halting steps took him to the wall. Five steps took him back. He turned, and said over his shoulder, "You do the same kind of work Frank did?"

"That's right."

"You do investigations for business firms and insurance companies?"

"We call them credit reports, or inspection reports," Webber said. "More than half of National Credit's business comes from life insurance companies."

Hendricks sat down again, and opened the briefcase. He pulled out a clipboard, with a stack of papers neatly attached. "These would be the reports Frank was working on today?"

Webber nodded.

"What's the next step?"

Webber answered mechanically. "The information is summarized in reports to the companies who ordered them. In the case of insurance companies, it provides a check on the facts the applicants furnish when they apply for insurance. And usually it gives the companies important supplemental information on the applicant's character, health, and financial positions."

"Is this some kind of personal shorthand that Frank used?"

"Yes. I use the same thing. Frank taught it to me. It's a big help in getting down information in a hurry."

Hendricks shoved the clipboard across the desk. "I'd like to have you look through these reports, and tell me if there's anything important there."

Webber leafed through the pages slowly. He glanced up once, saw the Old Man and Hendricks watching him intently, and grinned. They were after something, and it wouldn't occur to them that he might be better able to help them if they frankly told him what they wanted. Being police officers, they had to make a confounded mystery out of it.

"Frank always carried a big work-load," he said. He loosed the clip, and extracted one page. "I don't know if 'important' is the proper word, but this one is unusual. The rest are routine."

Hendricks took the paper. "Why is this unusual?"

"It's an application by a Miss Betty Parnet, you see, to the Star Mutual Life Insurance Company, for thirty-five thousand dollars' worth of life insurance. Even on the surface it looks unusual. It bothered Frank. We talked about it before we left the office this morning, and again at lunch. We usually eat—ate—a late lunch together, between one and one-thirty."

Hendricks said impatiently, "You didn't answer the question. Just what is there about it that's unusual?"

"It's a big hunk of insurance for a young, unmarried office worker. It might cost half of her salary. At first I thought it was a typing error. I had a case myself, a couple of months ago, where a young fellow had applied for five thousand. The typist made it fifty thousand."

Hendricks shifted his gaze to the ceiling, and his fingers resumed their silent tapping. The Old Man turned slowly in his chair, and sat looking out of the window at the darkened parking lot.

"You say at first you thought it was a typing error," Hendricks said. "What changed your mind?"

"I did after I talked with Frank at lunch. He'd checked with the Star Mutual Office. The amount was correct. But when he began his investigation—here, I'll read it." He read from Frank Milford's scribbled notes, filling out sentences to put it into presentable English. "Called at applicant's employers, Ronson and Wilcox. Receptionist stated applicant worked previous Saturday and had day off. Receptionist uncooperative. Called on applicant. She shares apartment with a Marilyn Andrews at address noted. Applicant Betty Parnet claimed to know nothing about a life insurance application. Stated flatly she had not applied for insurance. At one point slammed door. Acknowledged named beneficiary her uncle, stated she did not know him, wouldn't name him beneficiary if she did buy insurance. Application data confirmed. Identification positive."

Hendricks transferred his gaze from the ceiling to the floor. "What does he mean, 'Identification positive'?"

"He means he was satisfied that the person he talked with is the person described in the life insurance application—in other words, that he talked with Betty Parnet."

"All right. Would you mind reading that off again, for a Dictaphone?"

Webber read the notes a second time. The Old Man played it back when he'd finished, and Hendricks made scribbles in his notebook. "Will that do?" he asked.

"It'll do," the Old Man said.

Hendricks took a slip of paper from his pocket. "Does this mean anything to you?"

"Frank's writing," Webber said. "It looks like a license number, but I don't recognize it."

"He didn't say anything about it when you had lunch with him?"

"No."

"Did he tell you anything about this Parnet business that he doesn't have written down here?"

Webber shook his head. "No. We talked about it, and about what he ought to do. He thought he should talk it over with the boss, and have the boss check with the insurance company, before he went any further."

"Would you say Frank was a good investigator?"

"He was the best in our office. By far."

Hendricks took the report form, and carefully attached it to the clipboard. He sat back, his hands folded on the desk, his face thoughtful, as if he were phrasing and rephrasing a question in his head. "Just how do you interpret Frank's notes?" he asked finally.

Webber jerked erect. "The girl at the hospital!"

The Old Man got noisily to his feet. "He's real bright—a real credit to his family. If you dangle it in front of him carefully enough, and give him time enough, and finally hit him over the head with it, he's bound to get it. Real bright."

He strode toward the door.

Webber felt bruised and short of breath, as though he'd just received an unexpected kick in the stomach. He was still fighting to control himself when the Old Man growled, "I'll be home if anything turns up," reached for his hat, and left without a backward glance. He did not close the door gently.

CHAPTER TWO

Webber got up and walked over to the window. He stood looking down at the parking lot as the Old Man strode briskly over to his car, got in, and drove away.

Hendricks said quietly, "You two ought to bury the hatchet. You always used to be great pals."

Webber shrugged wearily, and returned to his chair. "The girl at the hospital," he said.

"Yes. The girl at the hospital was Betty Parnet. Now how do you interpret Frank's notes?"

"There's only one possible way to interpret them. Someone applied for an insurance policy on the life of Betty Parnet without her knowing about it."

"Is that possible?"

"It's possible to try. Obviously. I don't think it would be possible to get a policy issued. Certainly not one that large, with the investigating we do. In some circumstances I suppose a small one might slip through."

"I see."

Webber realized suddenly that Hendricks was an angry man. Fury throbbed in the scowl that twisted his lean face, and flashed dangerously in his dark eyes.

"How was Betty Parnet killed?" Webber asked.

"Automobile accident."

"Sure. Now I want you to draw me a nice, pretty picture, and don't spare the gruesome details."

"What sort of picture?"

"We have two people killed in two separate automobile accidents. You're behaving as if they're both murder cases. Start drawing."

Hendricks lit a cigarette, and tossed the match at an ash tray. He missed, and perched on the edge of the desk shaking his head. "Nerves. You and Frank were close friends, I suppose."

"He was like a big brother to me. A darned close big brother."

"He was a wonderful guy. I always wondered why he didn't marry. Some woman missed getting a first rate husband.

"Some woman missed being a young widow. Let's have it."

"We don't have any answers, yet," Hendricks said. "But I think I know what the questions are." He sent a smoke ring whirling across the room. "I have it figured out something like this. Frank had this Parnet investigation to do, and sometime this morning he went to the Ronson and Wilcox offices looking for her. She wasn't in. He tried to get some information from the receptionist, and she wouldn't talk. Is that unusual?"

"It happens," Webber said.

"Then Frank called on Betty Parnet at her home address, which is 974 Sunset Boulevard. He wrote up a summary of what happened and let the matter drop. I suppose he figured if Betty Parnet didn't apply for any insurance, of course the company wouldn't issue the policy, and he'd have been wasting time and money to go into it any further. He had plenty of other work to do, se he went ahead with his other investigations. Three of them concern people living in Rossville. Sometime late this afternoon he drove to Rossville, and when he'd finished he came back to Carter City on Ridge Road.

"From this point I'm guessing, but I think it happened this way. Earlier in the day, Frank noticed that he was being tailed. He wrote down the car's license number on his memo pad, probably meaning to ask me to check it out for him. Maybe he was just curious, or maybe he had a better reason. Whether or not he connected it with the Parnet case, we'll never know. But he did write it down.

"He drove back to Carter City, and just as he got to suicide curve he witnessed a peach of an accident. Or maybe he came along just after it happened. Anyway, it was a peculiar accident. According to witnesses, the car made no attempt to go around the curve. It went straight ahead, crashed through the guard railing, rolled down the embankment, and wrapped itself around a tree. The driver had her chest crushed and was probably killed instantly. Her face wasn't injured, and when Frank stopped and went over to the wreck, he recognized her as Betty Parnet.

"He knew something was wrong. The girl claimed she hadn't applied for any insurance, but somebody had, thirty-five thousand dollars' worth on her life, and she was dead. He drove a quarter of a mile toward town, and stopped at Bill's Place. Know it? Combination gas station and hamburger joint. Frank didn't drive into the station. He parked along the highway, and went in to make a phone call.

"Now get this. I've known Frank Milford all my life. We went through school together, and he went to work for National Credit about the same time I joined the force. We haven't been in close contact the past few years, but several times Frank has run into things he thought peculiar, and given me leads on them. His leads were always good.

"He had a lead for me today, Ron. As soon as he recognized Betty Parnet, he stopped at the first public telephone he saw and called me. Maybe he knew more about the case than what he wrote down. I think so—but unfortunately I was out. He left word that he was on his way down to see me, and then he ran out to get into his car. Just as he got the door open, a car veered off the road, ran him down, and kept on going. Witnesses said it had been parked up the road waiting. And they got the license number."

Hendricks paused, and puffed nervously on his cigarette. "We found the hit-and-run car abandoned. It was a stolen car, and the plates had been switched. Odd, the number of stolen cars we've had all of a sudden."

"You found the report on Betty Parnet in Frank's briefcase,

and started to add one and one," Webber suggested.

"Yes. We couldn't read Frank's shorthand, but of course the girl's name and address, and the information about the insurance policy, were typewritten at the top of the sheet. The fact that he stopped to call just after he passed the scene of the Parnet accident, and the fact that thirty-five grand is a fair amount of money, made us look into the Parnet death very carefully. The steering mechanism on her car had been tampered with. The poor kid didn't have a chance on that curve. She was murdered just as certainly as if someone had pointed a gun and pulled the trigger."

"Then there was that license number on Frank's memo pad. We already had the number of the hit-and-run car from witnesses, and they matched. When you find a hit-and-run victim who has already taken down the number of the car that killed him, you stop calling it an accident. Did Frank say anything at lunch about being tailed?"

"Not a thing."

"Either those men—there were two of them in the car— were following Parnet to see how things went, or they were still tailing Frank. They knew he'd talked to Parnet this morning, and the moment he walked over to the wreck to see the girl's body, he knew too much. Or maybe he knew too much anyway. They killed him the first chance they got. Total score: Two damned clever murders. If luck hadn't been on our side, both of them could have slipped through as accidents. Is that enough gruesome detail?"

"Plenty," Webber said.

"We have one more piece of highly interesting information. The car Betty Parnet was driving—that was a stolen car, too."

"You're kidding!"

Hendricks raised his right hand. "Fact."

"I've never seen a more unlikely-looking car thief."

"The whole situation is unlikely. The car she was driving was reported stolen at one-thirty this afternoon. The owner is one William J. Howard, who just happens to be Betty Parnet's uncle—and the man named as beneficiary on that insurance application. Before you start working that one over, I need some help. Betty Parnet said she didn't apply for an insurance policy. I have to know whether she was telling the truth, and if she was, the key problem is this investigation will be to find out who did. I've been trying to get in touch with the Star Mutual manager for the last two hours. No luck. How can I get ahold of that insurance agent tonight?"

"Just a moment," Webber said. "Can I have Frank's reports? I might as well type them up. If I don't, someone will have to go over the same ground again."

"Eventually they'll be evidence—I hope. I've already had them duplicated. Will the copies do?"

"I suppose."

"Take the copies, then. What about the insurance agent?"

"Your boys brought me down here," Webber said. "Will you drive?"

There was no moving traffic on Front Street, and few parked cars. Webber directed Hendricks into a parking place, they jumped out and quickly climbed a flight of stairs to the National Credit Company office.

Webber produced a key, fumbled, turned it over, fumbled again, and got the door open. "First time I've ever had to use it," he said.

Hendricks was studying the row of desks. "Did Frank have a desk here?"

Webber had a filing drawer open, fingering the contents. "Over there," he said, nodding. "The second one."

"Any chance that he got back here during the day, and left something in his desk?"

"No chance at all. He typed all of his reports at the apartment. Brought them in every morning, picked up his new assignments, and left for the day. If anything came up—here it is, Jones."

"Jones? Any first name?"

"No. Probably not necessary. Star Mutual probably has only one Jones."

"Carter City has more than one," Hendricks said. He flipped open a telephone book, and shook his head. "Carter City has about four columns of them. Can I make an outside call on this phone?"

"What are you going to do?"

"Put a man to work on the City Directory."

"We have six copies of it here."

Well down the list of Joneses, they located Raymond F., insurance agent. Hendricks telephoned, found him home, and promised to call on him within the next twenty minutes. He kept his voice down and spoke politely and somehow conveyed the impression that the consequences would be dire indeed if Mr. Jones did not see fit to wait.

He slammed the phone down. "Want to come along?"

"No," Webber said. Funeral arrangements, relatives—he wondered if Frank had left a will.

"I'm not just asking to be sociable. I might need you again."

Insurance policies. Bank accounts. Gloria. "All right. How could the police get along without conscientious citizens like me?"

When they reached the street they found a patrol car double-parked by Hendricks's car. "Any trouble?" the officer asked Hendricks. Hendricks told him no, no trouble, borrowed the use of his radio, and then sent him on his way. A moment later they were driving quickly through the near-deserted streets.

Hendricks drove staring moodily straight ahead. Webber leaned back and closed his eyes, and did his thinking aloud.

"There are other angles to this thing," he said. "You have an insurance application for a thirty-five thousand dollar policy, and there's only one person on this planet who could possibly benefit from such a policy. The beneficiary. William J. Howard, wasn't it? The girl's uncle? And if she was driving his car, and the steering mechanism had been tampered with—"

Hendricks made no comment.

"Wonder if there was a double indemnity clause," Webber mused. "That would double the amount of insurance in event of accidental death, which would make the policy worth seventy thousand. Few uncles have nieces who do as well for them. Have you done any checking on the beneficiary?"

Hendricks did not answer.

"Who is this guy Howard?"

"Like you say, there are other angles. Some of them are peculiar. How will the insurance company handle it?"

"That's hard to say. If no money was paid with the application, they'll just forget about it. But if money was paid, most companies consider the insurance in force when the examining doctor approves the applicant, if it's a large policy. Whether the company could legally avoid a payment on the basis of Frank's notes, I couldn't say, but you can count on a thorough investigation before Mr. Howard gets his thirty-five thousand dollars. Or his seventy thousand dollars."

"Was money paid with this application?"

"You'll have to ask agent Jones about that. Anyway, if Betty Parnet didn't apply for this insurance, she certainly didn't have a medical examination."

"But whoever did apply might have had an examination."

Webber whistled. "That wouldn't have occurred to my innocent mind. It takes a policeman to think up angles like that."

Hendricks spoke savagely. "A policeman—or a crook."

They had reached the outskirts of town, and Hendricks started checking the names of streets in a new subdivision. He found the one he wanted, and turned. He flashed his spotlight on a couple of house numbers, and drove slowly.

Webber made out outlines of a few of the houses and said dryly, "Insurance agents must do pretty well."

"This one seems to, if he can sell insurance to people without their knowing about it."

Hendricks checked again with his spotlight and parked. Webber followed him up the walk to a sprawling brick house. Chimes sounded as Hendricks raised the door knocker, and the door swung open immediately. The short, stocky insurance agent greeted them with a grin. It was a broad grin, a permanently-installed grin, a typical salesman grin. Webber had the feeling that he could meet such a grin on the street in Carter City, or in Moscow, or Timbuktu, and know a sales pitch was moving right behind it.

"Raymond F. Jones?" Hendricks said. "Hendricks is my name. I talked to you on the telephone. This is Ron Webber."

Webber handed him a card, and he glanced at it, and nodded. "Oh, yes. You do our inspection reports. Come in, won't you?"

They followed him into the living room, and caught a fleeting glimpse of Mrs. Jones disappearing into the kitchen. Jones flipped off the television set, and they arranged themselves on sleek, modernistic chairs that looked and felt as if they were folded for storage.

"What can I do for you?" Jones asked. He held onto the grin, but his feet were shifting at much too frequent intervals, and beads of perspiration glistened on his forehead. His thick glasses gave his eyes a comically-bulging appearance. Webber felt sorry for him. He hoped that the agent hadn't already spent his commission on Betty Parnet's application.

"We'd like some information," Hendricks said. "Recently you sold some insurance to a Miss Betty Parnet. Do you remember her?"

Jones relaxed visibly. He guffawed, and slapped his leg. "Remember her? I won't forget her in a hurry. I don't write a thirty-five thousand dollar case every day. In fact, that's the biggest one in a couple of months."

"An investigator talked with Miss Parnet this morning," Hendricks said. "She told him she hadn't applied for any insurance."

That wiped away the grin. "Hadn't applied—is this a gag?"

Hendricks shook his head slowly. Jones turned appealingly to Webber, who also shook his head slowly.

"The gal gave me an annual premium in advance," Jones said. "One thousand, five hundred and fifty-seven dollars and eighty-five cents. I won't forget that right away, either. You must have talked to the wrong person."

"Are you personally acquainted with her?" Hendricks asked.

"Never saw her before in my life. Some of us insurance agents have coffee together at the Carter Restaurant every morning at ten-thirty. I got there early, last Saturday, and the others hadn't come in yet. The waitress said to me, "How's the insurance business?' and I said, 'Fine' and then this gal came over to my table and said she wanted some insurance."

Webber glanced at Hendricks, and found him studying the polished brass trim around the fireplace.

"What's wrong with that?" Jones demanded. "There's no law against selling insurance to strangers."

"There doesn't have to be," Webber told him, "as long as we investigators do our job. What did she look like?"

"Blonde, average height, not bad looking."

Webber and Hendricks exchanged puzzled glances. It sounded like Betty Parnet.

"She didn't look particularly wealthy," Jones went on. "I thought she probably wanted a thousand dollars or two at the most. She said she wanted a savings plan, so I told her what five thousand would cost—just to sound her out, you know. Darned if she didn't ask me what thirty-five thousand would come to, and ten minutes later I had the application. Retirement plan at age sixty, with an annual premium."

"Was she carrying all that money around with her?" Hendricks asked.

"No. We went over to the First National Bank. I waited while she drew out the money, and she paid me, and I gave her a receipt."

"What about the medical examination?" Webber asked.

"The company requires two examinations for that much insurance, and they have to be on different days. I made an appointment for her for two o'clock Saturday, and another for nine o'clock Monday. Yesterday."

"Did she keep them?"

"I don't know. I suppose she did. Neither of the doctors has said anything. I offered to chauffeur her around, but she said she could manage all right by herself. Wait."

He bounded across the room to the telephone. It took him some time to locate both of his doctors, but he had recovered at least the front edge of his grin by the time he got back to his chair. "She kept them," he said. "She saw both doctors. I guess you must have talked to the wrong person."

Webber looked at Hendricks. "He wrote the application Saturday morning, and the first examination was Saturday afternoon. Remember Frank's notes? Betty Parnet wasn't working today because she'd worked last Saturday."

Hendricks face was grim. "That slipped my mind. Thanks."

"Look," Jones said. He got to his feet and stood with his hands on his hips. Anger colored his face. "No woman would pay that much money and take two examinations, and then say she'd never applied for any insurance. Women change their minds, sure, but I've never known one to forget a fifteen hundred dollar deposit. I'll see this Betty Parnet tomorrow, and prove you're wrong."

"You'll see her tonight," Hendricks said. "And so will your two doctors. And I hope you'll be able to prove something." He moved toward the telephone bench, and added, over his shoulder, "You'll have to see her at Municipal Hospital. I want to know if you can identify the body."

Looking at the insurance agent's stricken face, Webber pondered the mysteries of a police investigation. Hendricks attempted to hide his objective and spring it as a surprise—which was absurd, because the guilty party was forewarned anyway, and the innocent party not infrequently was able to perform simple arithmetic.

Webber wondered that the police ever got any information at all. They treated all their informants as suspects, and perhaps they treated their suspects as informants—never having been one, he didn't know.

But it was certain that few policemen would make good

insurance investigators.

Jones meekly gave Hendricks the telephone numbers where the doctors could be located, and Hendricks sat down at the telephone bench, tried to get his long legs arranged, and finally stood up to dial. He did not treat the doctors as suspects. He gave them a terse, professional statement of his problem, and then he called headquarters and arranged to have a stenographer at the hospital.

"There may be two Betty Parnets involved in this," he said, as he hung up. "We're not going to make much progress until we know which one was killed."

Jones got his grin adjusted while Hendricks was telephoning, and he began to cast glances of wistful speculation in Webber's direction.

"Been with National Credit long?" he asked, as they started for the door.

"Not long," Webber said.

"Are you married?"

"Not to my recollection."

At any moment Webber expected to hear him break out with that fatal line, "Mr. Webber, at what age do you plan to retire?" But the problem of transportation intervened. Jones insisted on driving himself, so that no one would have to be imposed upon to take him home.

"He's worried about the impression on the neighbors," Webber said, as he climbed into Hendricks's car.

"How's that?"

"He's afraid you might send him home in a patrol car, with siren screaming and a couple of uniformed officers as duo-chauffeurs. Speaking of home, would you drop me off at mine?"

"Sure. But I thought you'd want to find out what happens, for that report on Betty Parnet."

"You can telephone me, can't you?"

"Yes—"

"Do that," Webber said. "I'll be home. And awake.

Will, insurance policies, relatives, the funeral—he'd have to pick out an undertaker—and Gloria. *Someone* would have to tell Gloria.

Already the night seemed endlessly long, and he felt exhausted. And it was only the beginning.

CHAPTER THREE

Mrs. Cyrus Mahoney was an overly-plump, motherly indi-
vidual who had been worried about Webber from the day he
and Frank Milford rented an apartment from her. She thought
he worked too hard, and too-long hours, and that his lack of
height was somehow the result of an inadequate diet. At every
opportunity she contrived to feed him something.

She had been equally fond of Frank, and there was stark
tragedy in her face when she hurried forward to meet Webber.
"There's been a gentleman to see you," she said. "He came back
twice, so I let him wait." She jerked her head toward her living
room door.

"That was kind of you," Webber said, turning toward it.
"Thank you."

"It was on the radio. About Frank."

Webber clapped his hand to his forehead. Gloria would probably have heard, then. But perhaps it was better that way. He
stepped through the doorway, and a man he'd never seen before
rose to greet him.

"Mr. Webber?"

Webber nodded.

"I'm Jim Huss. City Engineer." They touched hands perfunc-
torily. "Wonder if I can have a few words with you."

"Of course." Mrs. Mahoney had vanished silently, a very neat
trick for one with her bulk. Webber saw no point in obliging the
man to walk upstairs, so he waved him back to the chair he had
been occupying, and seated himself on the sofa.

"I heard about—Frank Milford," Huss said. "I was shocked. For several reasons."

Webber nodded. Huss paused and looked away, seeming to find something fascinating about Mrs. Mahoney's battered piano. His appearance was colorless, if not nondescript. His trousers were not baggy, but neither were they sharply pressed. His stooped shoulders and rimless bifocals suggested that he spent his days peering at blueprints. He was slender, but with an incongruous hint of a paunch. Webber noted the streaks of grey in his hair, and guessed his age as fifty-five.

And he was plainly uncertain of himself, if not embarrassed. His voice was soft, his words halting. "Shocked," he said again.

Webber's curiosity was almost overbalanced by the tasks ahead of him. He waited silently, his mind on funeral arrangements, and notifying relatives, and searching Frank's papers for a will and insurance policies. It would complicate matters if Frank had a safe deposit box, but Webber couldn't recall him ever mentioning one.

Huss turned back to Webber and looked away again. He said, almost apologetically, "You see, Frank Milford was working for me."

"Really? What sort of work?"

"An investigation."

"Strange he never mentioned it," Webber said.

"I asked him not to mention it to anyone. It was strictly confidential."

"I see."

"Now I'm wondering—well, it seemed pretty certain, from what the police said, that he was run down deliberately. I'm wondering if it could have had anything to do with—well—"

"Your investigation?"

Huss nodded.

"Since I don't know anything about your investigation, I'm afraid I can't help you. I'd suggest that you bring the matter to the attention of the police. Immediately."

"I was also wondering if he'd left any notes, or records, of what he was working on."

"I'll have to go through his papers," Webber said. "I can look. But wait—I'd have to have some idea of what to look for."

"Yes." Huss was studying the piano again. "I don't suppose it would be possible for me to—well, look—"

"I don't suppose so," Webber said firmly. "I'm not familiar with the legal complications, but eventually there'll be an executor, either court-appointed or named in a will, and if you think anything among Frank's personal effects might be your property, you apply to him for it."

"But you said you had to go through his papers."

"Only to see if he left a will, and to see if there are any relatives who should be notified. That sort of thing."

"I see."

"So I'm afraid I can't help you."

"Can I rely on your discretion?"

"Within reason," Webber said. "If I were to turn up anything relating to Frank's death, I'd have to turn it over to the police."

"Of course. I didn't mean that kind of discretion. It's just that there's been too much loose talk already. There have been some nasty rumors about fraud in city construction contracts. I asked Frank Milford to investigate them—the rumors, not the fraud. We've investigated the possibility of fraud ourselves two years ago—investigated thoroughly. Mayor Kambas even hired a team of outside engineers to conduct an independent investigation. There's no basis for the rumors, but they persist. Obviously they're politically motivated. If we could find out where they're coming from, we could put a stop to them."

"When you hired Frank, did you tell him that the job might be dangerous?"

Huss shook his head. "It never occurred to me. But as soon as I heard he'd been killed—deliberately—why then I thought if he'd turned up information exposing certain people—"

"You may be right," Webber said slowly. "A car followed Frank all afternoon, waiting for an opportunity." And by coincidence, the opportunity occurred when he stopped to telephone

Hendricks. An ironic break for the murderers of Betty Parnet, whose murder might have gone undetected if Frank Milford had died sooner—or later.

"I'll be on the lookout," Webber said. "I'll let you know if I find anything."

"Thank you."

Webber showed Huss to the door, thanked Mrs. Mahoney again and wearily climbed the stairs to the apartment he had shared with Frank Milford. The telephone was ringing when he opened the door. It was Bob Hendricks.

"None of them recognized her," he said. "The doctors can say positively that the girl they examined wasn't Betty Parnet, because they have their examination records. The real Betty Parnet has no operation scars. The girl they examined had an appendectomy. The real Betty Parnet is almost an inch taller. There are a couple more details like that. There'll be the signature on the application to check, too. But there isn't any doubt that someone has a shrewd scheme worked out. A girl who looks a little like our Betty, but not enough so that any of the three has the slightest doubt about it, applied for a whopping amount of insurance under the name of Betty Parnet, and got herself examined by two different doctors under the name of Betty Parnet. Frank Milford—what's that again?"

"Know a man named Jim Huss?"

"City engineer. Sure."

"He's tossed a monkey wrench into your case," Webber said, and told him about the conversation with Huss.

"I've heard the rumors," Hendricks said, "or heard of them. How long has Frank been working on this special assignment?"

"I didn't think to ask Huss."

"If you turn up anything in his papers, I want to know about it. Until then, I'll be satisfied with the way I have this one blocked out. Frank saw the Parnet accident, tried to tell me something about it, and got killed. Anything else?"

"No. I've a few other things—"

"You aren't the only one who has reports to write," Hendricks said and hung up.

Webber went to Frank Milford's desk and punched the switch on the fluorescent desk lamp. He seated himself, and as the light came on he leaned forward to admire the rich, polished surface of a pipe that occupied a central place of honor among the dozen or so pipes that crowded the pipe rack. Poised on the edge of the bowl was a small angel, its thumb firmly in place against its nose in the time-honored gesture of disdain. It was Frank Milford's favorite pipe, polished frequently with loving care and never smoked. It never had been smoked.

"Your halo looks rusty," Webber said with a grin.

He remembered a heated argument with Milford over whether the little figure was really an angel with something impish in its disposition, or a devil masquerading as an angel. Webber had voted for the devil; Milford held out for the impish disposition.

"It's perfectly obvious," he had said. "It's saying, 'I'm in heaven, and to hell with you.'"

Now that Frank was dead, Webber felt ready to concede the angel. The little figure seemed a personification of Frank's own character: pure in heart, but with a perplexing veneer of impishness.

"I think," Webber said to the angel, "that I'm going to have to steal you. I'm entitled to some kind of a memento to remember Frank by."

He wondered if, behind that expressive hand, the angel was sticking out its tongue. He returned it to the pipe rack, lit a cigarette, and wearily went to work on Frank Milford's desk. In a bottom drawer, in a plump manila envelope, Webber found a last will and testament, a ten-thousand dollar life insurance policy, and a bulging package of government bonds. The insurance policy named one Maude Milford as beneficiary. The bonds named only Frank Milford.

Webber opened the insurance policy to the Photostat of the application, and found Maude Milford identified as Frank's aunt, with a Chicago address. He glanced casually at the will and was surprised to find himself appointed as executor, with the request that he handle last expenses in an economical manner, dispose of personal property as he might see fit, and donate any cash remaining from bonds and savings account to a worthy charity. College football scholarships and homes for retired prostitutes were not to be considered as worthy charity.

Webber grinned at the angel. "So I won't have to steal you."

The angel's gesture clearly implied that it made no difference.

Webber went to the telephone, and after some sparring with Chicago information, learned that Mrs. Milford had no telephone listed. Another Milford did, at the given address. Webber took the number and got the call placed. While the distant telephone rang unanswered, he raised his sleeve to look at his watch. It was twenty minutes after ten. He blinked in surprise, closed his eyes tiredly. The longest night he could remember was still young.

Finally a man's voice responded. The operator said briskly, "Person to person for Maude Milford."

"My God!" he exclaimed, and muttered in a low aside, "It's for mother." There was a babbling uncertainty in the background. "Just a moment," he said. "Carter City, you say? Maybe—I'll see—"

Webber waited uncomfortably, watching his watch. A minute went by—two minutes. Suddenly there was a voice, old and tired. Immeasurably tired.

"Hello?"

"Maude Milford?" the operator asked.

"Yes."

"Go ahead."

Webber said "Hello."

"Hello. Is this Frank?"

"I'm a friend of Frank's, Mrs. Milford. I'm sorry I have to tell you this. Frank has been killed in an automobile accident."

"Oh," she said dully. "Oh dear."

The receiver fell with a crash. Confusion welled up around the telephone, and the man's voice returned. "Couldn't you have told me? Did you have to call at this damned hour?"

"Sorry," Webber said. "I had to notify somebody, and her name was the only one I found in Frank's stuff."

"I see. What was it you wanted?"

"Arrangements have to be made. I can look after them myself, but if Frank has any relatives who would prefer to do it—"

He left the sentence unfinished.

"I see. Frank didn't have any relatives except our family— none that I know about, anyway. Mother took care of him after his own mother died. That was in Carter City. We haven't seen him for years, but I guess he and mother wrote now and then."

"Then you have no objection to my looking after things?"

"Gosh, no. Mother is an invalid. She couldn't come down there, and she wouldn't be any help if she did. I doubt if my wife or I could get away."

"Are there any other relatives who should be notified?"

"My sisters, maybe. Both of them are in California."

"Should I call them? Or send them telegrams?"

"That won't be necessary. I'll let them know."

"All right." Webber said. "I'll take care of things. The funeral will probably be the end of the week. I'll send you a telegram as soon as I know."

"That shouldn't be necessary. But—all right. We probably won't be able to get away. And say, did Frank have insurance, or enough money to handle things?"

"I don't think there'll be any problem there."

"Well, good. Fine. Thanks for letting us know."

"Please convey my sympathy to your mother," Webber said dryly.

He hung up. Across the room, the angel was leering fiendishly.

Webber thought for a moment, dialed Police Headquarters, where genial Sergeant Pete Adams was on the desk. "Pete," Webber said, "I need some fatherly advice."

"So? Haven't you got a father?"

"I have to look after the funeral arrangements for Frank

Milford, and I lack experience. Can you recommend an undertaker in the medium low-price field? I want the thing respectable, but I don't want someone who specializes in platinum caskets."

"Mmm—know just what you mean. Clark Brothers, I think. They're out on Lake Street. Just a moment—I'll get the address."

"I can look it up. Thanks loads, Pete."

"Any old time. You got something you want buried just call me."

Webber called Clark Brothers, and got a grumpy response that brightened wonderfully with the awareness that a customer was on the telephone.

"Tonight," Webber said. "Right now. Immediately." He didn't want Frank Milford left in the sterile indifference of that hospital room a minute longer than necessary.

"Certainly, sir," Clark Brothers said easily. "We'll be at the hospital in twenty minutes."

Webber hung up, and thumbed his nose at the angel. He took the copies of Milford's reports to his own desk, and glanced through them.

Except for the Parnet case, they were all for small life insurance applications—several for ten thousand, the rest for less. Routine stuff. Webber shook his head in admiration as he looked them over. Milford had gone after every one of them as if a quarter of a million was at stake, and what an investigator he was! Good natured and friendly, with a sly sense of humor, he loved people and he loved talking to people. By the time he finished with a hostile housewife she was telling him things she wouldn't tell her own husband.

It came through in every line of his scribbled notes. This woman had a nervous breakdown five years ago. This man has a heart condition. Sees his doctor on the sly, and hasn't told his family. X runs a roofing repair business in his spare time—broke his leg in a fall two years ago. Y spends her leisure hours at home with a bottle. Little things that would loom large under the careful scrutiny of a life insurance underwriter.

And fortunately not common things. The overwhelming majority of life insurance applicants, Webber knew, were readily insurable and had nothing to hide. Among the minority, some were completely honest, and some held out on the general premise that what the insurance company didn't know wouldn't hurt it. The company knew perfectly well that what it didn't know could hurt it badly. So there were investigations.

He looked carefully at every line for a misplaced clue, for anything that would tie in with the Parnet case, but there was nothing. Finally he pulled his typewriter toward him, and started typing.

The telephone rang. "Ron." a voice said. "I want to see you."

Bells, and singing, and a hint of perfume vibrating in every word.

"Gloria!" he exclaimed. "Have you—heard?"

"I heard. Ruth called. She heard it on the radio. I want to see you. Now."

"Where?" Webber asked.

"Here."

"No," Webber said firmly.

"Perhaps you're right, perhaps—do you know the Crow Bar?"

"By its reputation—which isn't good."

"I'll meet you there. In half an hour."

"All right."

It was a dive. A juke box pounded out a rhythmic blare, a slatternly waitress with a soiled white apron gave Webber a sly wink, and at least two of the arguments along the long bar threatened to end in violence. The hefty bartender was keeping an eye on both, but he managed to give Webber a long stare.

She was seated in a booth at the back of the room. He had dreaded this meeting as only a man can dread any kind of a reunion with the false partner of his first love affair. He was mildly surprised to find that he could face her with irritation, rather than regret; and with fatigue, rather than instant ardor.

She was wearing sun glasses, which seemed a ridiculous gesture. Her hair was as blond as he remembered it, which meant that she'd dyed it—again. The last time he'd seen her, from afar, she'd been a brunette. The lovely curve of her cheek, the tiny mole on her chin, the quaintly turned-up nose that gave her always the aspect of a whimsical little girl, the urgent thrust of her breasts—all that was hauntingly familiar. And yet she had changed. She had gained weight. Her eyebrows were painted at a more rakish angle. Her mouth—but surely that couldn't have changed!

Gazing at her blankly, he realized the he was really seeing her for the first time. A vampire, Frank Milford had called her. "Drop her, Ron, while you still have some blood left." And when Webber ignored him Milford cut him out with such deft ease that the humiliation still burned in spite of the close friendship they developed later.

And she was a vampire. Milford brought him her diary to read, which cured him effectively and permanently. Neither of them ever mentioned her again. Webber had not even been certain that Milford was still seeing her.

"What are you drinking?" he asked.

"Beer," she said.

"Will you have another?"

She shook her head. He ordered beer for himself, and as the waitress flounced away she leaned forward and asked urgently, "Did you do it, Ron?"

He stared at her. "Do what?"

"Kill Frank?"

He was too flabbergasted to answer. They regarded each other silently until the waitress brought Webber's beer.

"You can tell me," she purred.

"Don't be ridiculous," he said. "Why on earth would I want to kill Frank?"

"I understand perfectly. Why should you deny it?"

Webber took a deep breath. She actually thought he'd murdered Frank for her! "I haven't any doubt that Frank was murdered," he said. He'd accepted that she was a vampire, but that measure of colossal conceit was new to him. "But if there was a girl involved her name was Betty Parnet—not Gloria Lardie. And he was killed because of an insurance investigation, not a love affair. I spent a good part of this evening with the police."

"Then they suspect you. It doesn't surprise me."

"It would surprise me if they suspected me. I was helping them. I'm an insurance investigator, too—or had you forgotten?"

"They turned you loose. I'm glad. But you can't fool *me!*"

He stared at her again. "This is a ridiculous waste of time for both of us," he said. "But I'm glad I came. You can think anything you like—and I don't care what it is. Its worth something to know that. When did you see Frank last?"

She did not answer. He was searching his own memory. He'd paid very little attention to Milford's comings and goings, but when he thought about it, it seemed a long time since Frank had made an enigmatic telephone call—or had a late date.

"He'd dropped you, didn't he?" he asked.

She lurched forward, upsetting her glass, and slapped his face resoundingly. He mopped the table with paper napkins, and did not even look up as she stalked away.

Almost before the sharp click of her spike heels had receded someone slid into the booth in her place. Webber glanced up in surprise, and met the saddest pair of eyes he had ever seen. It was a man, weirdly tall and slender, wearing a black suit with white shirt and black bow tie. He looked even more out of place in the Crow Bar than Webber felt.

He said softly, "Good evening, Mr. Webber."

"Have we met before?" Webber asked.

"To my intense regret, no."

"Then how'd you happen to know my name?"

He gave Webber a smile. "I make it my business to know things—and people. There's really only one name that interests me tonight, and a short time ago you used it—Betty Parnet."

"You were eavesdropping," Webber said.

"That is a manifestly improper accusation. My hearing is excellent, and your syllabifications were clearly audible at least four booths away. Your young lady is, I fear, a pronounced schizophrenic with paranoid tendencies, and I prognosticate an unhappy future for her."

"She isn't so young anymore," Webber said. "That may be part of her trouble."

"Indubitably. But though I do not hesitate to frankly delineate a female's mental condition, I rarely feel at ease in discussing her age. There is a difference between objective reasoning and sheer speculation. You mentioned Betty Parnet."

"Did I?"

The man leaned forward, and his voice lost its lightness and became as cold and hard as burnished metal. "I have a compelling certitude, Master Webber that you know far more than I do about today's tragic events. You may even know more than I'll be able to find out. But I can see that this is the wrong time to ask for confidences, Master Webber. Do you wish to congratulate me on my patience?"

Webber shook his head. "I'm too busy being amazed at mine."

A fleeting smile touched the gaunt face. "I'll be seeing you, Master Webber!"

He walked away slowly, leaving Webber twiddling his thumbs in perplexity. He drained his glass and decided to have another beer, but before he could summon the waitress another man slid easily into the booth opposite him. That face, at least, was familiar—a detective Webber had known since he was a child.

"What'd Pronk want?" he asked softly.

"Who's Pronk?" Webber asked

"He was."

"Nick Falcone's right-hand man?"

"Or his brains, or his number-one stooge. Have it any way you like it."

"He sounded like a professor from a girls' seminary."

"That he is not," the detective said fervently. "I love him for his own sake. He's unique. He never got through high school, so he's making up for it by memorizing the Encyclopedia Britannica. He knows everything there is to know through the letter M, but he only talks like a professor when he has time to think what he's going to say. I can think of a thousand better things to do than tailing him, but orders are orders. Your dad won't sleep nights until he's rid the town of both him and Falcone—which must mean he's had insomnia for twenty years, and as far as I can see it's due to last for another twenty. We thought we had Pronk cold a week ago, but it was the old story of the disappearing numbers slips. What'd he want?"

Webber looked at him levelly. If Carter City's vice lord and his henchman were interested in Betty Parnet, the case was developing angles far beyond the ken of an ordinary detective. Or an insurance investigator. It could mean that the insurance fraud was somehow tied in with a bigger racket.

"If you see Bob Hendricks," he said, "tell him that Pronk is interested."

"You mean that auto accident thing? Interested how?"

"Just—interested, Webber said. "He didn't specify."

"Thanks. I'll tell him."

"He won't thank you," Webber called after him.

He ordered his second beer, and drank it, and then he drove home. It was after midnight, and he had at least two hours of work ahead of him, typing Frank Milford's reports and his own.

CHAPTER FOUR

Webber reached the National Credit Company office before seven, and found the outer office deserted. The door of the boss's private office was closed, which meant that he was in. J. Russell Boyd was one of those unfortunate individuals who are human dynamos until two in the afternoon, when they quietly fade away. The office force had often speculated as to just what time Boyd turned up for work in the morning, but none of them had ever gotten up early enough to find out.

Webber knocked, and Boyd called cheerfully, "Come in."

He was a grandfatherly sort of person, bald headed with a little grey fluff above his ears, a plump, good-natured face, and horn-rimmed glasses that he seemed to use mainly for carrying and pointing. This time Webber surprised him with the glasses on, but he whipped them off and innocently put them to work scratching his head as he blinked at Webber in mild surprise.

"A little early, aren't you, Ron?"

Webber eased himself into a chair. "Just a little."

"I heard about Frank. I'm more sorry than I can tell you."

"Yes," Webber said. "We'll miss him."

"In more ways than one. He was more than just a good investigator."

Boyd looked away while his hands fussed with his glasses, and Webber learned back and closed his eyes. He told himself that he should go home and go to bed, but he knew he wouldn't be able to sleep.

"It looks as if you've had it," Boyd said. "Want to take the day off?"

Webber blinked himself awake. "No. I may have to take some time off to make the funeral arrangements for Frank, but otherwise I'll be all right. I typed up the inspections he did yesterday. I wanted to talk to you about this Parnet report."

"Parnet? Oh—Parnet. That was the thirty-five thousand case, wasn't it? I've already looked it over. It looks clean."

Webber leaned forward. "Would you say that again, please?"

"I said I'd already looked at it." Suddenly his expression was no longer good-natured. He gazed steadily at Webber, a frown clouding his face. "Is something wrong?"

"Only that the report hasn't been turned in yet. I have it here."

Boyd straightened up stiffly in his cushioned chair, produced a pipe from a desk drawer, and made a drawn-out ceremony of getting it packed and lit. "Let's have a look," he said.

He shuffled through the stack of papers on his desk, found the one he was looking for, and shoved it at Webber. "Greenway's initials," he said. "But *now* I remember giving that one to Frank. How did Greenway get in on it?"

"I couldn't say."

"I wonder if the Star Mutual people slipped up, and requisitioned the same report twice. I don't remember seeing more than one requisition. I don't suppose Greenway's come in yet."

Webber opened the door, and glanced into the outer office. "Not yet."

Boyd played absently with his glasses. "I'll have to find out how Greenway got onto the case without my knowing about it. What is there about this Parnet application that's bothering you?"

"According to Frank's notes, the girl said she hadn't applied for any insurance."

Boyd snatched at Greenway's report. "Something's wrong somewhere. Greenway interviewed her. It looks all right."

"Frank didn't make mistakes."

"None of my men make that kind of mistake," Boyd said sharply. "Do you have Frank's report here?"

"As far as he went," Webber said, handing it to him. "He didn't finish it. He was going to talk to you about it first."

Boyd nodded, and placed the two reports side by side. "Odd." He leaned over the desk to stare at them. "Damned odd, wouldn't you say? But it should be easy enough to clear up."

"Ordinarily it would be. But Betty Parnet is dead."

Boyd started. He propelled his chair backwards with one firm push, and swiveled around to look out of the window. "Parnet. I heard that on the radio this morning, but it didn't register. That alters the situation. Star Mutual—I'll give them a call." He glanced at the clock. "But it wouldn't be any use before nine. The girl told Frank she hadn't applied for any insurance, but when Greenway interviewed her—"

"Evidently Greenway saw the same girl the doctors and insurance agent saw," Webber said. "And that girl wasn't Betty Parnet."

Boyd turned back to his desk, and leaned forward with his hands folded. "Suppose you start at the beginning."

Webber told him about the interview with the insurance agent, and the failure of the agent and the two doctors to identify the dead girl. He added a summary of Hendricks's conclusions on the case, and Boyd's face was grim when he finished.

"Were they certain about the identification? I mean, the accident could have messed up her face."

"It didn't, though. And the doctors had their examination records to check. There isn't any chance of a mistake."

"Then it's a clear-cut case of fraud. And you think the girl Greenway interviewed wasn't Betty Parnet?"

"I don't see how it was managed, but it certainly looks that way."

Boyd tapped the report. "Either that, or this was planted on us. Either way I don't understand it. I want to see Greenway as soon as he comes in."

"The police will want to know about this second report. Do you mind if I tell them?"

"Go ahead. And you wait for Greenway, and bring him in as

soon as he gets here."

Hendricks arrived first, striding quickly across the room and leaning over Webber's desk. "I got the message," he said impatiently. "What's up?"

Webber told him about the two inspections reports, and Hendricks sat down at the next desk, tilted back, and made himself at home with both long legs draped familiarly over the desk top. "Correct me if I'm wrong," he said. "Whomever engineered this thing had an intimate knowledge of the life insurance business."

"No correction."

"I doubt if the average person is even vaguely aware of the investigating that goes on when someone applies for life insurance. Take me. I wouldn't have any idea about how to get a phony report into this office."

"I wouldn't, either," Webber said, "unless I made it myself."

"Who is Greenway?"

"Ralph Greenway. He's been with National Credit a long time—Fifteen years, at least. Forty-five, married, flock of kids. As far as I know, he's a good investigator. He covers a lot of ground."

"Honest?"

"He wouldn't last fifteen years here if he wasn't. I can't say that I know him well. He's not what you'd call a friendly person. Speaks only when spoken to—that sort of thing."

"When will he be in?"

"Around eight."

"Just introduce me," Hendricks said. "I'll see the he's spoken to."

Greenway walked in at a quarter to eight. He gave Webber a nod, sat down at his desk, and emptied his briefcase. Webber got up and walked toward him, suddenly aware that he disliked the man. Mainly it was because he looked the way most people would expect an investigator to look—a slight, drab man, wearing a loose-fitting, baggy suit. He seemed completely out of place away from a crowd to lose himself in.

Webber introduced Hendricks. Greenway shook hands indifferently, muttered something about hearing about Frank, and wasn't it too bad, and now the whole staff would be overworked until a new man could be broken in.

"The boss wants to see you," Webber said.

Greenway got up without a word, and shuffled toward Boyd's office. Webber and Hendricks followed him in, and he watched Webber introduce Hendricks to Boyd without a flicker of curiosity showing on his face.

Boyd shoved the inspection report at Greenway. "Is this yours?"

Greenway glanced at it, and nodded.

Hendricks reached over and took the report. "I'd like to ask some questions."

Boyd looked at him resentfully. He was, Webber thought, all coiled up to land on Greenway with both feet, and he was not welcoming Hendricks's intrusion.

"Certainly," Boyd said, and swiveled around to stare out of the window.

"First, I'd like to know how these investigations get started. What's the procedure?"

Boyd answered politely, but he kept his eyes on the window. "When an agent obtains an application for insurance, he turns it in at his branch office, and someone there prepares the requisition for the investigation. It is mailed to us at our post office box, and we pick up that mail three times a day."

"Then anyone could fill out a requisition, and mail it to your post office box."

Boyd turned slowly. "Yes and no. The requisition forms are printed up with the name of the insurance company and its account number. Anyone who knew how to use a typewriter could request a report, if the proper form were used. But I can't see why anyone would want to bother, unless it was out of some perverted notion of embarrassing the insurance company, or costing it money. All of our reports are mailed directly to the insurance company's home office."

"I see," Hendricks said. "At least, I think I see. Now let's talk about this report."

Boyd said quickly, "Ralph, where did the requisition for this report come from?"

Greenway answered almost indifferently. "Doris. I stopped in to do some directory work late Monday afternoon. She handed it to me. She said a special messenger had brought it over, and it had to be done as quickly as possible. I did as much as I could that evening, and finished it in the morning."

"What time Monday?"

"About four-thirty."

"It was after I left, then," Boyd said. "Odd Doris didn't mention it to me the next day, but I suppose it slipped her mind. Another requisition must have been in the afternoon mail, and I processed it the next morning and assigned it to Frank. At least we know that there were two requisitions. The branch office must have made a mistake."

"I'll check on that," Hendricks said. "Greenway, you interviewed someone you thought was Betty Parnet. I'd like to hear about that."

Greenway picked up the report. "The girl was sitting on the front porch at this address—974 Sunset Boulevard. She asked if I was looking for someone, and I said for Betty Parnet, and she said that was her. So I asked the usual questions. That was all there was to it."

"And she convinced you she was Betty Parnet?"

Greenway shrugged. "She knew her birth date, and where she was born, and where she lived last. She knew her employer and her last employer. She said she'd applied for the insurance, and she knew the company, and how much insurance. She knew the beneficiary was her uncle, and she said he was helping her pay for the insurance."

"In other words," Webber broke in, "she knew everything that the girl who applied for the insurance knew."

Greenway turned to Boyd. "Is there anything wrong? I mean

why all this fuss about a report?"

"It's a long story," Boyd said, "and the fact that Betty Parnet was killed yesterday doesn't make it any less complicated."

Greenway's icy calm remained unbroken. He said, "Oh."

"Just a moment," Webber said.

He'd a thought, or a half-thought, that seemed to light everything up clearly for a moment, and then pass. He backed up uncertainly and found a chair in the corner, and struggled to work it out. An official requisition and an unofficial requisition. The U.S. Mails and a special messenger. Two investigators, Greenway and Frank Milford.

When he looked up the three of them were staring at him. "What is it?" Hendricks asked finally.

"It's the matter of timing."

Hendricks nodded. "I've been wondering about that. Go ahead."

"Jones wrote that application on a Saturday morning. We'll have to find out when he turned in the application to his branch office. Whenever it was, it didn't get processed until Monday. The regular requisition was mailed late that morning or early that afternoon."

"Right," Boyd said. "It must have been in the late afternoon mail, so it didn't get any attention until Tuesday morning."

"Then you assigned it to Frank. But this other requisition came in by messenger, and because it was purportedly an urgent matter and because Ralph happened to be here, he went to work on it right away. Supposing Ralph had finished it Monday evening, and had turned in a complete report on Tuesday morning?"

"If I'd seen it in time, I'd have assumed that the branch office made a mistake, and I'd have called Frank off."

"Right. I think that was what was supposed to happen. Ralph was supposed to have the report completed by yesterday morning."

Greenway protested. "I couldn't have. Not on an application for that much insurance. People weren't available. You know yourself—"

"I know," Weber said. "You know. But whoever sent that requisition by messenger didn't know."

Hendricks stepped over to look out of the window, and Boyd obligingly moved aside. "If Greenway's report had come in soon enough," Hendricks said, "then Frank wouldn't have made his investigation. Greenway's report would have been sent off to the company, and we probably wouldn't have known that the real Betty Parnet never applied for that insurance. And the insurance company would have been stuck with paying the thirty-five grand."

"In that case," Boyd said, "why didn't they send the special messenger on Monday morning? Did they know that the agent didn't turn in the application in time for a requisition to be mailed from the branch office on Saturday?" He looked at Webber. "It's a matter of timing, but I'd say that their timing wasn't very good. They fluffed it."

"Not necessarily," Webber said. "Ralph, if you'd gotten the requisition earlier in the day, where would you have gone first?"

"To her place of employment, probably," Greenway said. "But by the time I got away from here I knew it would be closed, so I went there the next morning."

"Right. If you'd gone to Ronson and Wilcox on Monday, you'd have met the real Betty Parnet, and the scheme would have been blown. By having the special messenger arrive here just before closing time, they made certain that you'd go to the home address first—where the fake Betty Parnet was waiting on the porch. And that you'd go to Ronson and Wilcox on Tuesday—*when Betty Parnet had the day off.*"

Boyd's sudden intake of breath whistled audibly.

"I'd like to borrow Greenway," Hendricks said. "I want to know if he can identify Betty Parnet."

"Of course," Boyd said. "Whatever you think is necessary." He turned to Webber. "You mentioned something about a funeral arrangement for Frank?"

"Yes. The sooner the better, I suppose."

"Could you do that now? I'll get the Star Mutual home office on the phone as soon as I can catch anyone there. I'm certain that they will want a death inspection report. If I were them, I'd want every possible angle looked into. You can get to work on that as soon as you're free. Better phone in first, though."

Hendricks borrowed Boyd's telephone, and called headquarters. He said little and did an inordinate amount of listening. Then he took his leave of Boyd, and went out with Greenway trailing after him. Webber followed them.

"If you don't mind, I'll tag along," he said.

"I thought you were allergic to that hospital room."

"I am."

Hendricks paused in the act of lighting a cigarette. "So?"

"So what? You aren't going to pull a Gestapo, and force me to view the body, again. Or are you?"

Hendricks shook his head. "No. I thought maybe you knew something, and I was wondering who tipped you off. The girl isn't at the hospital any longer. Her uncle had her removed."

With each of them driving their own car, they made a small procession through Carter City's rush hour traffic, and cleared the business district after a dreary succession of red lights. Hendricks stepped his speed up to forty. Webber, bringing up the rear, hoped the boys from the traffic squad wouldn't pick him off and think he was trading on his relationship with the Old Man.

Traffic thinned out as they neared the edge of town, and the parking lot of the Fairview Garden Chapel was deserted. Greenway followed Hendricks up the walk, and Webber paused for a moment to stare at the building. As a strictly non-connoisseur of funerals, he had never taken a close look at it.

It gave him the overwhelming impression that only the very wealthy could afford to die. The building had a fine old southern-colonial front, a feature as native to Carter City as a Chinese temple. A sprawling, single-story wing had been added at the rear, with a superabundance of glass brick and a miniature veranda with miniature pillars at the side entrance.

"And it's just as well that they added that wing at the rear," Webber mused, "Because one look at it, and the original mansion would have turned its back."

The grounds were a sweep of bright green grass and carefully nurtured shrubbery and flower beds. Someone with a passion for geometry had laid out a network of crisscrossing walks, and statuary and fountains were piled up in an imposing manner at the intersections. Through the shrubbery he sighted the broad back of a gardener, who was propelling a wheel barrow across the parking lot, hoses coiled about both arms.

Webber tried to conjure up a picture of Frank Milford enjoying his last rites in such a setting, and failed. Frank would be horrified, or—no. He would be immensely amused. He would laugh in the startled mortician's face, trip the pall bearers, and ever thereafter haunt the garden paths.

Grinning broadly, Webber hurried after Hendricks and Greenway. He caught up with them as they were going through the door, took one startled look at the interior, and whistled softly.

"The girl's uncle is picking up the check," Hendricks said.

"With the insurance money?"

Hendricks's muttered response was inaudible. He led Greenway away, and Webber paced solemnly around a tinkling fountain while he waited. His feet sank deeply into the intertwined flowers of a carpet that would have set him back the best part of a year's salary. Soft strains of music made delicate sound patterns in the air. He did some mental calculations based on what he had assumed to be Carter City's death rate, and decided that the proprietor of the Fairview Garden Chapel worked on the basis of large unit profits.

A few minutes later he caught a glimpse of Greenway leaving by the side entrance. He started after him, thought better of it, and resumed his pacing. An elderly man and woman came in, were met by a sedate, black-suited attendant, and ushered away. Webber stopped his pacing and sat down in what he hoped was an attitude of appropriate reverence.

Hendricks came out, finally, sat down beside Webber, and studied the fountain. "What do you make of it?"

"Just one thing. I can't afford to die."

Hendricks smothered a laugh with his hand, and jerked his head toward the door. Webber followed him back to the parking lot. He followed him because he couldn't keep up without running, and he guessed that running would be one of the many things that were not done in the grounds of the Fairview Garden Chapel.

"Get in my car," Hendricks said. "We can talk for a minute."

Webber climbed in beside him, and watched while Hendricks lit a cigarette and carefully deposited the match in the ashtray.

"Little grains of evidence," he murmured.

"You must be feeling pretty good. Normally you don't wax poetic before noon."

"I'll feel good about this when I see the murderer—or murderers—being led into the courtroom. And I'm going to be there to see it."

"What about Greenway?"

Hendricks shot a mouthful of smoke at the windshield, and watched its curling rebound. "He never saw the girl before. As you said, the element of timing was important. Or—"

"Or what?"

"I don't know. I'm going to do some checking on friend Greenway. Odd isn't it that he just happened to be there when that messenger arrived? Are investigators usually in the office at that time of day?"

"Now and then. Catching one on a particular day would be a long shot."

"And if he hadn't been there, the rush requisition wouldn't have been handled until the next day."

Webber nodded.

"Interesting. When a coincidence fits a plan so obviously, it's always interesting. Well—we have two murders, a thirty-five thousand dollar motive that isn't going to benefit anyone, two stolen cars, and some slight-of-hand about an insurance application. Can you pick a suspect out of that mess?"

"We also have something about frauds in city contracts, and a possible underworld connection."

"Yes. But I'm not worried about either of those things—yet."

"They don't fit?"

Hendricks shook his head. "I can appreciate Jim Huss being upset about it. He asked a man to do a delicate investigation, and the guy turned up murdered. Not knowing about the insurance application, he would naturally jump to the conclusion that his investigation was involved. I can understand Prof Pronk's curiosity too. There have been rumors, lately, that Carter City's underworld has been hosting some non-resident talent. If it isn't at Nick Falcone's invitation, he's resenting it."

"What could that have to do with it?"

"The stolen cars. Those two men who ran down Frank Milford. If whoever engineered the Parnet thing imported thugs to do the dirty work, Big Nick is naturally wondering who is making free on his preserves. What Big Nick wonders, the Prof finds out. No, the underworld connection doesn't worry me—yet. It might even be a help. If Big Nick is sufficiently resentful, we can expect some anonymous tips—if the Prof comes up with anything."

"This William J. Howard is still the only one who could profit from the insurance."

"Yeah. That's another odd one. Uncle William reports his car stolen, and we find his niece in it, dead. And she—or somebody—has just applied for a big chunk of insurance in favor of Uncle William. It's almost too obvious, isn't it?"

"I've heard of murder being done for less."

"Then there's the matter of the fifteen hundred plus dollars paid on the life insurance application. Betty Parnet never had that much money. She did have about three hundred dollars in the bank, and she drew it out yesterday afternoon."

"You're working fast," Webber said. "You must have had breakfast with a bank president."

Hendricks grinned. "At the time of her death, she had seven

dollars and forty-two cents in her purse. We're trying to find out what happened to the three hundred."

"The agent said he waited at the bank while the girl—"

"Oh, sure. He waited by the door, and the girl went up to the window and came back and paid him the money. What she did at the window is anybody's guess. Maybe she just got change for a quarter. I've asked the bank to check its Saturday withdrawals to see who, if anyone, withdrew something like the amount of that insurance premium. I don't expect them to find anything."

"Just what do you think of the chances that the uncle planned all this?" Webber asked.

Hendricks laughed. "I don't think anything. I just have spasms of curiosity. There's the motive to consider. A man who commits murder for money usually needs money. As far as we can find out, Howard doesn't. He owns stocks and bonds in quantity, he was president of his own company until he retired last year, and he still keeps an office uptown and works as a consulting engineer when he feels like it. He has large chunks of cash in all the local banks and savings and loan associations. He's a conservative investor. He's made his money and held onto it. Somehow I can't see him murdering his niece or anyone else for money."

"What does Howard have to say about it?"

"Another odd coincidence. Mr. Howard left town on business yesterday afternoon—shortly after he reported his car stolen. Which gives him a first-rate alibi. We got ahold of him in New York about midnight. His first reaction was, 'So what?' He didn't have any kind of a relationship with his niece. He seemed only vaguely aware that he had a niece."

Webber jerked a thumb at the Fairview Garden Chapel. "So what?"

"Well—he did some thinking after we talked with him, and decided to make like a favorite uncle. Betty Parnet didn't have any other relatives in these parts."

"When does Howard get back?"

"Shortly after noon, today."

Webber opened the door, and got out. "Okay. Maybe I'll have a talk with him."

"You're welcome. He's a hard-boiled old geezer. You'll find him about as sentimental as a slide rule. By the way, the Old Man wants to see you."

"Business or pleasure?"

"He's not getting any more pleasure out of this than I am."

"I'll look him up at my earliest convenience."

"Better make it early," Hendricks said.

Hendricks drove off, and Webber returned to his own car and headed across town to the Clark Brothers Funeral Home. The facilities were less than palatial, but adequate. One of the elderly Brothers Clark greeted him with polite sympathy and made himself helpful in a manner that was kind and only moderately mournful. Webber went through the necessary motions, and made the necessary decisions, and Frank Milford was standing beside him all the way, his usual impish satiric self.

So Webber selected a casket.

"It's just a box, Ron. I won't be uncomfortable if the padding isn't thick."

And made arrangements for interment.

"I'd prefer a hole in the back yard, Ron. A cemetery is no place for a man who enjoys privacy."

And picked out a marker.

"I want a big one, Ron, old boy. And make it say, 'Do Not Disturb. Leave all letters and telegrams with the room clerk.'"

With the time of the funeral set, and arrangements made to notify Frank's relatives, Webber's leave-taking was less a departure than a frantic rush to escape. He stopped at a drug store to telephone the National Credit Office. Boyd told him to get on with the Parnet death inspection.

"How deep do I dig?"

"It isn't enough to know that the girl didn't apply for insurance. We'll have to be able to prove it—in court, if it comes to that. Dig until you hit bottom."

Webber telephoned William J. Howard's office, and

persuaded his secretary to schedule an appointment for him for four o'clock. Then he drove over to police headquarters to see the Old Man.

He was kept waiting for ten minutes, and when he entered, the Chief of Police was not alone. Mayor George Kambas, looking more the bald-headed businessman than the silver-thatched politician, grinned at Webber and said, "So this is the young man. Jim Huss told me he called on you last night."

Webber nodded.

"Jim means well, but he's a fool. We don't need an investigation to know who these guttersnipes are. Did you find anything?"

"Find—oh. In Frank Milford's papers. No I didn't find anything. To tell the truth, I haven't really looked, yet."

"You won't find anything," Kambas said. "There's nothing about this for an investigator to get his hands on. Just dirty politics. And I don't think they killed your friend. They wouldn't have the guts for that. They aren't birds of prey, they're vultures. Nice meeting you, son. Glad you have things under control, Chief. I'll drop around again...."

He was gone. Webber gazed blankly at the open door. "What was that all about?"

"There's a city election next spring," the Old Man said. "Evidently the politicking is starting early. What's on your mind?"

"Nothing I'd want to burden the police with. Bob gave me what I thought was an invitation, if not a summons. What's on your mind?"

"Bob says you're going to do some kind of an investigation on the Parnet business."

"I am."

"Why?"

"Because I work for a living, and the boss told me to."

The Old Man dropped into his chair, and got out a cigar. He clamped his teeth on it, and spoke sideways at Webber. "How many men does Boyd want to lose? Oh, don't look so blamed innocent. Whoever killed Frank Milford didn't do it for practice. The people behind this thing aren't playing for fun; give the marbles back when the game is over. An amateur would get in the way of the police, and stand a good chance of ending up dead."

"How may of your men do you expect to loose?"

"That's entirely different. My men are trained to take care of themselves. They're armed. They know what they're up against, and they won't take any chances. They'll be working in pairs. I wouldn't even turn an experienced detective loose to run down a killer on his own."

"You've got your wires crossed," Webber said. "I won't be looking for your killer. The insurance company will accept the police reports on that. What I'm interested in is Betty Parnet's application for insurance."

"That's all Frank Milford was interested in, wasn't it? You might be lucky enough to stumble onto something, or interested parties might think you've stumbled onto something, and they'll be interested in seeing that you don't pass the information along."

"Thanks for the warning. If I stumble onto anything I'll let you know."

"I'll have a talk with Boyd about this."

"Do that," Webber said. "I'm sure he'll promise his full cooperation. But don't make the mistake of trying to tell him how to run his business. He has some ideas of his own about professional standards, and he might tell you a few things about amateurs on the policy payroll."

"What are you going to do?"

"I have a date with Betty Parnet."

It didn't come out quite the way he meant it. He remembered as he went out the door that Betty Parnet was lying in state at the Fairview Garden Chapel, and for all its plush furnishings, that was not an appropriate place for a date.

CHAPTER FIVE

Ronson and Wilcox, Attorneys, occupied a suite of offices on the fourth floor of the National Bank Building. Webber walked slowly past rooms 402 and 404, both of which were marked *Private*, and entered 406. The door conveniently closed itself after him.

He paused to give the room a quick appraisal. The conservative furnishings were obviously expensive, the office girls good looking, and there were several clients waiting. The firm was thriving, and Webber instantly placed its proprietors in the elite class of prospective customers of the Fairview Garden Chapel.

The receptionist, who was also the switchboard operator, smiled a bland, mechanical smile. She was perhaps thirty, and she looked as if she'd had her sex appeal on display for so long that it had weathered away. She still had a frosty kind of attractiveness, but what she lacked in youth and freshness, she tried to compensate with stylish clothes and cosmetics. Webber decided that is was a poor exchange.

But the woman interested him. If she were the same receptionist who'd been on duty the day before, she'd given very little information to Greenway and even less to Frank Milford. It was possible that she didn't like investigators; it was also possible that she knew something about Betty Parnet that she didn't care to divulge.

It was no ordinary inspection report that Webber was working on. Applicants for life insurance did not often die before a policy was issued, and on the rare occasions when they did, most companies followed a procedure that was both logical and reasonable: They proceeded as if nothing had happened. They assembled their usual underwriting information, and if the applicant qualified for the insurance and had paid the first premium with the application, they issued the policy and paid the claim. If the applicant did not qualify, they rejected the application exactly as they would have had the applicant been alive, and returned the premium.

Webber thus had two overlapping problems to consider: Betty Parnet and her eligibility for thirty-five thousand dollars' worth of life insurance; and the suspected application, which included the two medical examinations. The first had already been investigated by Greenway, but Webber would amplify Greenway's information if he could.

He exchanged smiles with the receptionist, and said, "Good Morning. You knew Betty Parnet, didn't you?"

Her eyes widened. She half turned, looked about the office as if appealing for help, and murmured, "Again?"

"Again?" Webber echoed, feigning puzzlement.

"Yesterday morning there were two men asking questions about Betty, one right after the other, and then—"

"Yes," Webber said. "She applied for a life insurance policy, you see. And now that there will be a death claim on the insurance policy, there has to be another investigation. Do you mind?"

Her hands fluttered nervously as she handled an incoming call. Webber waited; puzzled by the way she kept her eyes on him. When she had finished he flashed what he hoped was a melting smile.

"The questions are quite simple. Like—did you know Betty personally?"

"I suppose you could say that."

"How long had you known her?"

"Ever since she started working here. Six or seven months."

"So you know how old she was?"

"Twenty-two. Maybe twenty-three."

Webber nodded understandingly. She was beginning to relax,

but he sensed a deep-seated resentment, or perhaps even an inexplicable fright, that might snap back on him at the slightest misstep. "Did Betty have any income apart from her job here?"

She smirked. "Why would she work here if she did?"

Webber smiled, and she smiled back, which was a good sign. Sometimes people warmed up and sometimes they froze up, but he never failed to be awed at the way people were polite to a prying stranger. Most people, that is.

"Was Betty in good health?"

She shrugged. "As far as I know."

"Did she ever have any sickness?"

"Not since she came to work here. She never missed a day of work, except when she had a day off."

"She had yesterday off, didn't she?"

She hesitated. He thought she would ask him how he knew, but she said, "Yes. That was because she worked Saturday."

"I see," Webber said. Clearly Ronson and Wilcox were enlightened employers. Not many businessmen, he thought, would give an office girl a day off merely because she put in some overtime. He wondered if Betty Parnet's relationship with one of her bosses was something more than that of an office girl. That would account for days off and large insurance policies.

Except that Betty Parnet hadn't applied for any insurance. As for the rest, he would see.

"Did Betty use intoxicating beverages?"

"Now and then, I suppose."

"Did she smoke?"

"No."

"Did you ever see her intoxicated, or hear of her being intoxicated?"

She scowled—a danger sign. "Certainly not."

He risked one more question. "Did she ever have creditors bothering her?"

Her head jerked back, her eyebrows tilted, and she snapped the answer. "No!"

Webber decided on an orderly retreat. He said, "Thank you

very much, Miss—"

"Johnson. Ruth Johnson."

He moved quickly away, and left her staring after him. He would have given something to know which investigator she had talked to first, the day before. Greenway, he thought, and that would explain why Frank Milford had found her uncooperative.

Later he might have to make the acquaintance of other office girls at Ronson and Wilcox, and perhaps even have a few words with the bosses; but he would postpone that, against the chance that he might turn up something specific that he wanted to ask them about.

In an uncomplimentary way, Sunset Boulevard was sometimes called Millionaires' Row. At one time it had housed Carter City's wealthy families, but now the large houses were converted to apartments or rooming houses. The porches sagged dismally, the paint was peeling, and the once neatly trimmed shrubs were maintaining a scraggly battle for survival. It was still a pleasant, winding street, with large shade trees and several small parks.

Webber drove along slowly until he found 974, a grimy, foreboding old house with an unkempt yard. He crossed the wide porch, and inspected the doorbells. A neatly typed card informed him that Betty Parnet and Marilyn Andrews occupied apartment number two. He rang the bell.

There was no response. He tried apartment number one, and then number three. He could hear the bell ringing in number three, which made it the front apartment, and also made him wonder why landlords never numbered their apartments while sober. Invariably apartment number one was tucked away out of sight and almost out of human ken, in the basement, attic, or somewhere at the rear with a camouflaged door.

He caught a flicker of movement through the glass, and stepped back as the door swung open.

It was a wan-looking woman, aged anywhere from the mid-thirties to the mid-forties. She wasn't dressed for company. Her house dress was torn, patched, dirty and wet. Her hair hadn't met up with a comb that morning. There were soap suds on her hands, and through the open door of her apartment he could hear the steady thumping of a washing machine.

Webber had her name from the scribbled card above her bell. He said, "Mrs. Warren?"

She admitted it, and stood watching him suspiciously. A small boy, perhaps four years old, peeked timidly around her and ducked back out of sight. Webber introduced himself. He gave her his card. He explained his errand and smiled his best smile, and talked fast to get across the idea that he would be eternally grateful for a few simple answers to a few simple questions.

She invited him in, and got him seated on a worn sofa that sagged to an alarming proximity with the floor when he sat down. She went to turn off the washing machine, and returned with two cups of coffee. She ceremoniously served sugar and canned milk. Webber asked her if he was pale enough for her to guess that he'd missed breakfast that morning, and she smiled and went back for some cake. It was homemade cake, and surprisingly good. Webber guessed that he was an element of excitement on a day when she obviously hadn't expected any. She seemed grateful.

"Betty was a real nice girl," she said. "It's a terrible thing."

The boy crept out of a corner and edged onto the far end of the sofa. He sat gaping at Webber.

"Bobby will miss her," she said. "She was wonderful to him. Always bringing him things, and looking after him sometimes when I went shopping. Marilyn, too. I suppose she'll move away, now. We'll miss both of them"

"Did Miss Parnet have any friends?" Webber asked.

"Oh, yes." She hesitated and looked at him doubtfully. "I mean, she had lots of friends around here. I suppose you mean men friends. I don't think I saw a man call for her all the time she lived here."

"That seems odd," Webber said. "She was young, and reasonably attractive."

"She was real nice looking—her and Marilyn, too. I've wondered about that. I'd 'a thought they could have had dozens of fellows if they'd wanted them. I guess they just didn't want them. Sometimes of an evening they'd go for a little walk down to one of the parks and back. I've seen young fellows driving by stop and try to talk to them, but they wouldn't have nothing to do with them."

"Miss Parnet must have gotten along well with Miss Andrews."

"Real well. They worked at the same place, so they went to work together and came home together, and they always went places together. They had the back apartment, and they were always doing things to fix it up. Putting up new curtains, or painting, or building shelves. They enjoyed themselves more with that old apartment than a lot of people would with a new house."

Webber moved easily into his routine questions, and got voluminous answers. Betty Parnet's health was excellent. She had not been ill in Mrs. Warren's recollection. She was a thrifty person—paid all her bills promptly and was practically immune to salesmen. There was an insurance agent who called on her and Miss Andrews several times in a vain effort to underwrite their futures. Mrs. Warren knew, because the agent was the same one she had the children's insurance with. The two girls believed in paying cash, and their only charge account was with the milkman, who collected every two weeks. They left the money with Mrs. Warren.

As for drinking, neither of them would touch the stuff, even in its milder forms. "I know," Mrs. Warren said. "Ed—that's my husband, Ed—sometimes he gets a case of beer for over the weekend. We could use the money for something else, but I guess as long as he don't do anything worse than drink beer I can't complain. He likes to sit out there on the porch and drink beer and listen to the ball game. Many a time I've seen him offer those girls a bottle of beer, and neither one would take any. I never saw anything in their apartment but fruit juice. They drank a lot of that."

"Did Betty ever mention an uncle of hers, a William J. Howard?"

She was silent for a moment. "I don't think so."

"Did you happen to be home Monday evening—say between four and six?"

She threw up her hands. "I'm always home."

"Did you notice a girl sitting on the front porch about that time?"

Her surprise was obvious. "Why, yes. I did." She started to say something—ask a question perhaps—hesitated, and went on with a rush. "She said she was looking for Betty and Marilyn. I told her the girls usually get home about five thirty, so she asked me if it was all right to wait for them. I invited her in, but she said no, she'd just wait on the porch. The next time I looked out she was gone. The girls didn't get home until late. They said they ate with some friends and went to a movie. They were wondering who she was, too."

Webber gave her an understanding nod, and kept his excitement to himself. It had been almost too much to hope for confirmation of Greenway's story, but there it was—someone knew the girls would be getting home late, and by having the phony requisition delivered just when they did, they gave themselves a good chance that an investigator would be along while the phony Betty Parnet was waiting. It had been the best kind of gamble—one that could be made without any risk at all. If the girls had arrived home unexpectedly, the impostress would probably have been selling cosmetics, or offered some similarly safe line. It had almost worked. Someone knew a great deal about the insurance business—but not quite enough.

It also meant Greenway had told the truth, that he could be in no way implicated. Webber felt strangely relieved at that, and wondered why.

Mrs. Warren got out a handkerchief, and blew her nose violently. "It's such a terrible thing," she said. "Betty was talking for weeks about getting a car, and she was so happy all day yesterday. And then to think that the first ride she took in it—"

Webber was on his feet when he interrupted her. It took some effort to dig himself out of that sofa, but he made it. "You mean she *bought* that car?"

"Yes. She asked Ed about it, and he said it was a real good buy if it was in good condition. So she went down town yesterday and got her money from the bank, and the man brought the car over a little after five. She wanted to bring it when Ed was here, so Ed could look at it. Ed said it was a steal at that price, so she bought it and went for a ride to try it out. That was the last time I saw her."

Webber sank back onto the sofa. "I see," he said. He saw a lot—too much. Six blocks down Sunset Boulevard, and then Betty Parnet had turned south onto Miller Street. A mile or so farther out Miller Street became Ridge Road. Carter City had annexed a big chunk of the surrounding countryside a few years before, but it had never gotten around to renaming Ridge Road. So Miller Street suddenly became Ridge Road well inside the city limits, to the mutual confusion of everyone.

Betty Parnet's steering apparatus had gotten her around the corner onto Miller Street, but the next sharp turn she had to make was Suicide Curve. As an inexperienced driver with a fancy new toy, she was probably going faster than she should have been. Suicide Curve was a bad place to be driving fast, even when the steering apparatus was working. The experienced driver took a firm grip on the steering wheel, slowed to twenty-five, and maybe prayed a little. After one ride around that curve at normal speed, the inexperienced driver was either deeply experienced or in the hospital.

She hadn't had a chance.

As far as Webber knew, the police were keeping it quiet about the accident being a murder, so he sat submerged in the sofa, and had another cup of coffee, and exchanged a little small talk with Mrs. Warren.

Obviously Betty Parnet was a girl of sterling character, well-liked by everyone, quiet, kind, attractive—kind of a universal blueprint for anyone's favorite sister. She was also dead. Her death had been worth something to someone, thirty-five grand, perhaps, and another murder when Frank Milford got in the way. Webber reminded himself that murder was a police job, and his business was an insurance application. Mrs. Warren was having to blow her nose more frequently, so he thanked her for the information, cake and coffee, slipped the boy a piece of gum, and departed.

He drew a blank at the other apartments, so he tried the neighbors. A sickly-looking man whom Webber could tell at a glance was a poor insurance risk slammed the door in his face. At the next house, an elderly woman thought she knew who Betty Parnet was, but she couldn't remember ever talking to her. Even that information was worth something. Betty Parnet had been living there long enough for scandals to work their way two houses down the street, if there were any.

On the other side of 974 he found two women who'd had Betty Parnet baby-sit for them. They described her in glowing terms. Across the street he had another lucky break. A jovial, plump, middle-aged man admitted to knowing Betty Parnet well. In fact, he'd given her driving lessons when she decided to buy a car.

"She was a careful driver," he said. "On a narrow road she'd drive the people behind her nuts by keeping way under the speed limit. I know she would have been careful on Suicide Curve, because we went out that way a few times. I just don't understand how it happened."

Webber did, but he kept the information to himself. "What sort of a person was she?"

"She was a fine girl. Smart. She learned fast. When I taught my wife how to drive, we were at it for six months. Edna had to have her learners permit renewed twice. All Betty needed was a few minutes behind the wheel, and she was doing everything right.

Back in his car, Webber sat there for a few minutes thinking over the report he would have to write. Any well-managed insurance company was by nature a cautious institution. It had to be cautious, even to the point of being suspicious. Contrary to rumors that circulated constantly, it did not investigate claims in the hope of cheating its customers. It investigated to keep itself from being cheated.

Although all of the evidence indicated that Betty Parnet's application was fraudulent. Webber's job was to collect all the pertinent facts, check them for accuracy, verify them in any way he thought necessary, and write a report that would enable the insurance company to reach a clear-cut decision. Neither the insurance company's decision, nor its thirty-five thousand dollars, was any concern of his. He, and the National Credit Company could not gain if the company rejected the claim, and could not lose if the claim were paid. The insurance company paid them for the time spent in gathering information, whether or not the nature of the information pleased the insurance company.

He checked his notes. Before moving to the apartment on Sunset Boulevard, Betty Parnet had lived at an address on Charles Street. As Webber pulled away from the curb, he glanced at the rear-view mirror. A block down the street, a blue sedan pulled out and moved slowly after him. He stepped down on the accelerator, watching it carefully. He quickly widened his lead. He was three blocks ahead when he reached Miller Avenue. As he turned left, he glanced back over his shoulder. The sedan was already picking up speed. When it turned left onto Miller, it was only a block behind him.

"Slick operator," Webber mused. But he had to be certain. He pulled over to the curb, parked, and—remembering what had happened to Frank Milford—carefully got out of the car on the right side. He went into a small grocery store and bought a pack of cigarettes.

The sedan was nowhere in sight when he started out again, but in the next block he saw it parked, and he caught a passing glimpse of two men in the front seat. He had never seen either of them before.

At the first stop light he carefully recorded the license number in his notebook, grinning delightedly at the thought of Bob Hendricks's apoplectic reaction were he to find a second victim of a hit-and-run accident who had taken down the license number of the car that hit him.

He thought he could shake the car easily in the confused traffic of the business district. He managed a sudden turn onto Broad Street, and gave his car a burst of speed. The sedan was still with him.

"A real slick operator," Webber murmured admiringly. "In fact, an expert. Now—we'll see."

He reduced his speed, and the sedan came on boldly. He speeded up, and opened distance between them. At Green Circle he made a quick right turn and shot around the curve, hoping to God there wouldn't be any kids playing in the street. He completed the half-circle at Broad Street, and his luck held. The traffic was clear. The sedan wasn't in sight. Webber ignored a stop sign, and gunned his car across Broad and into the other half of the circle. He drove on around, parked out of sight of Broad Street, and walked to the corner.

The sedan had emerged from the first half of the circle, and stopped. Its driver was obviously befuddled. Finally he turned right, and raced away out Broad Street.

Webber chuckled. "Very interesting. In fact, fascinating."

He went back to his car, and drove toward the business district. At the first drugstore he parked and telephoned police headquarters. He asked for Bob Hendricks.

"A blue sedan following me," he said. "Two men in it. Thought you might like to know."

"Sure. License number? Make?

Webber gave him the license number. "They all look alike to me," he said. "It's a couple of years old."

"Fine investigator you are!"

"Well—automobiles don't usually apply for life insurance. Let me put it this way. Supposing you were tailing somebody out Broad, and he got cute and pulled into Green Circle. What would you do?"

"I'd back into a driveway on Broad, and see what way he went when he came out."

"Right. Now this boy is clever. I took him through traffic, and he didn't lose ten feet. But he followed me into Green Circle, and I went all the way around and lost him."

"Interesting."

"Yes. He's slick, but he isn't too familiar with Carter City. You mentioned a rumor about out-of-town talent. I thought you'd like to know."

"Thanks. And Ron—are you sure you lost him?"

"The last time I saw him he was headed east on Broad. I'm going west."

"Take care of yourself."

"One thing more. Did you know Betty Parnet *bought* her uncle's car?"

"No. I didn't know that."

"See a Mrs. Warren. The Sunset Boulevard address. She loves to talk."

"Right," Hendricks said, and added a second time, "Take care of yourself."

Webber laughed. "I've got myself in good hands."

He had not driven half a block before a blue sedan pulled out from the curb and followed him.

Webber swore softly as he watched the car being maneuvered expertly through traffic behind him. "Figured he'd lost me, so he started back west, and there was my car parked at the curb. This is the most stupid one I've pulled yet. Good hands, I said!"

He decided to ignore it, though he drove back through the business district as recklessly as he dared. He turned right onto Miller Avenue, passed four cars with a burst of speed, and looked back just in time to see the blue sedan execute a neat maneuver and slide into the right-hand lane two cars behind him.

"He doesn't know Carter City," Webber told himself, "and he didn't learn that technique in Carter City. So what do I do with him?

Losing him would be no problem. As a kid Webber had spent enough time at headquarters and in patrol cars to know every street and alley of Carter City. "But it might be interesting," he thought, "to see just what he's up to."

He drove breezily out Miller to Southwick, and followed Southwick through to Charles. His admiration for the driver of the sedan increased block by block. He actually kept his car out of sight part of the time, and when Webber turned onto Charles he deliberately drove on past. A few minutes later, as Webber was parking in front of the Charles Street address, the sedan drove slowly across the next intersection. Webber resisted the temptation to wave.

It was an older residential district of small houses, and this one was neat and well-kept, with flowers and a freshly-mown lawn. Webber's surmise was that the owners were an older couple, augmenting income or pension by tasking in a roomer or two. It was after eleven, and he had an early lunch on his mind as he walked up to the door.

An elderly lady jerked the door open before he could touch the bell. Grey-haired and grim-mouthed, she aimed a pointed nose in his direction and scowled. The overall effect was formidable.

"I don't want any," she said.

Webber smiled. "Then it's a good thing I'm not selling anything." He introduced himself, and patiently explained that he wasn't a peddler. Did she remember Betty Parnet? She did. Could she spare him a few minutes to talk about Betty Parnet? She doubted it. He withstood her withering gaze boldly, and eventually she backed away from the door and invited him in.

She hobbled on ahead of him, using a heavy cane. He followed her through an enclosed porch and into the living room, and she motioned him onto the sofa. The sofa did not sag. It looked as if it had never been sat on. She circled once around the room, and straightened a doily on the back of her chair before she sat down.

"I know you," she said. "You're Webber's boy."

Webber admitted it without blushing.

"Are you working for the police?"

"No," Webber said. "We cooperate with the police, of course, but otherwise any information we collect is absolutely confidential. National Credit is a private, independent company. The police can make you answer questions. We can't."

She delivered a resonant snort. "Like to see a policeman make me answer questions."

"So would I," Webber said with a smile. "How did you happen to know me?"

"There aren't many people in this town I don't know. Oh, I don't mean all the riffraff that's been drifting in lately. But I know all the old families. I knew your dad when he was just a pup. He was a rough one. Never thought he'd amount to anything." She looked at Webber sternly. "I'm not sure that he has. What's this about Betty Parnet?"

Webber started his line about a routine investigation, and she cut him off with a wave of her cane. "I heard about her being killed. I can't say that it surprised me—not one bit. I'll go to her funeral, of course. It's the Christian thing to do. But it didn't surprise me. Such goings on—in a respectable neighborhood too. If she'd been my daughter, I'd have paddled her good. I thought she was a nice, quiet girl when she moved in. Then all of a sudden she started keeping company with that crook Falcone. I warned her. She wouldn't listen to me. Just a nice old man, she said. Humph! It's not easy to pull the wool over my eyes."

Webber sat up very straight. "Falcone? Not—Nick Falcone?"

"The very same. Lots of decent, law-abiding people in this town have never heard of him, but I have, and with your daddy being Chief of Police I think that you have, too. He's a no-good scoundrel. I told her, but she wouldn't listen to me. And then one night he brought her home drunk. Well! That was the last straw. I made it perfectly plain to her—one more time and out she went. A week later she gave me notice, and I haven't seen her since."

"You're certain it was Nick Falcone she was going with?"

"Just as certain as I was that you're Ronny Webber's boy. I may be an old woman, but there's nothing wrong with my eyesight. She had that crook calling for her here, and she even had the nerve to introduce him to me. I never would have thought it when she moved in here. I've had girls rooming with me for years, and I'm a good judge of character. It wasn't my first mistake, though. I had two sisters rooming here once, and one of them—but that's another story. I could tell you tales about some of our so-called prominent citizens that would curl your ears. If a girl wants to be a kept woman, that's her business, but she's not going to be kept in my house!"

Before Webber could catch his breath and ask another question, she changed the subject. "There was a fellow here Monday evening asking questions about Betty. Do you know him?"

"Mr. Greenway?"

"He didn't tell me his name. Fishy-looking fellow. Needed a haircut and a clean shirt."

Webber smiled. "That was Mr. Greenway. Did you tell him about Nick Falcone, and about Betty coming home drunk?"

"I certainly did not. I'd hoped she'd mended her ways, and if she did I wasn't going to throw dirt at her. If she didn't, there's plenty of others that would. He wouldn't need my contribution. I didn't tell him much of anything."

"But you don't mind telling me?"

"That's different. I kind of know you. Anyway she's dead, and what I say now won't hurt her."

"Did she go out often with Nick Falcone?"

"I'd call it going steady. Once or twice a week, for quite a while. The last time was when he brought her home drunk, she was pretty sick, and I told him to his face he wasn't to set foot in my house again, and he didn't. I suppose she met him somewhere else."

"How long did Betty stay with you?"

"Lets see. She was new in town. Came from out of the state

somewhere—a little town in Wisconsin, I think. She never said much about it. I had my room listed at the YWCA, and they sent her to me. That would be—yes. The best part of a year she stayed here. She moved out last January."

Webber recorded the date in his notebook, so he could work out a timetable—not that he expected to learn anything from it. "Did she go out with any other men?"

"Not a one. Not that I ever found out about. There's a nice clean-cut young fellow down the street who was crazy about her, and she wouldn't have anything to do with him. She seemed like such a nice girl when she moved in, too. But as I said, she wasn't my first mistake. Her getting killed like that didn't surprise me. Do you know if she was drunk?"

"She wasn't drunk," Webber said.

She seemed almost disappointed.

Webber thanked her, and noted down her name which was Mrs. Charlotte Lamont. She escorted him to the door, and told him to remind his dad about the time she caught him stealing her father's apples, and paddled him.

Halfway down her front steps, Webber turned. "There's one thing you might like to know."

"What's that?"

"After Betty left here, she did mend her ways."

The blue sedan was waiting down the street, and it took Webber just four blocks and two alley short-cuts to shake them completely. He drove back to the business district, left his car at the city parking lot at Second and High, and walked over to Main Street. A newsboy thrust a paper into his hand, so he paid him and backed up against a storefront to look at the front page.

Betty Parnet's death was listed as accidental. Frank Milford's death was listed as accidental—hit-and-run variety. Some industrious reporter had turned up a picture of Betty Parnet, and it was on page one. It was a snapshot, but it was quite good. It almost looked like her.

Or perhaps the Betty Parnet Webber had seen in the hospital death room almost looked like the snapshot.

The picture gave him an idea. He tucked the paper under his arm and walked past the Ace Grill, where he had planned to eat, and turned in at the Carter Restaurant.

It was five minutes to twelve. The noon-hour rush was already underway, but Webber found an empty table toward the rear, and a waitress had a glass of water in front of him when he got himself seated. He complimented her on her speed and dexterity, and she modestly said it was nothing at all.

"Were you working last Saturday?" Webber asked.

She told him she worked every day except Tuesday, when the restaurant was closed. Webber held up the picture of Betty Parnet.

"Ever see her before?"

"Yes," she said. "She ate here now and then. Not very often, but sometimes a whole crowd of girls comes in from those offices in the bank building."

"Do you know an insurance agent named Jones?"

"Short, fat fellow? Sure. A mob of insurance agents comes in every morning, for coffee."

"Last Saturday Jones came in early, and talked to a girl about insurance. Did you happen to see them?"

"Sure. The place was practically deserted. He sold her an insurance policy."

Webber pointed at Betty Parnet's picture. "Was that the girl he talked to?"

"Oh no!"

"You certain about that?"

"Sure. I knew this Parnet. I didn't know her name, but I'd seen her quite a few times. And this other girl—the one Jones sold the insurance to—I know her, too. I don't know her name, but she used to eat in here a lot."

Webber asked the waitress for her name, and recorded it in his notebook. The little lady didn't know it, but she'd just earned herself a dollar tip.

He concentrated on the menu, and when he looked up to give his order a familiar face was approaching. Webber leaped out of his chair, and intercepted it.

"Hello, Miss Johnson," he said.

He recognized the look that she gave him. As a boy in high school, he'd had a friend who collected insects, and Webber had seen that look on his face every time he found a new specimen.

"Would you care to join me?" he asked. He pulled out a chair, and stood waiting. She did not react enthusiastically, but at least she didn't run away, either. She sat down in the constrained manner of one who was too tired to walk any further.

Webber, who had missed not only breakfast, but dinner the night before, ordered a steak. Ruth Johnson selected a salad plate. Their conversation proceeded along similar lines. In response to his full-bodied remarks, Miss Johnson nibbled around the edges of her lettuce. She also kept her eyes on her plate, as if one more glance at Webber's face might ruin her appetite permanently. Webber knew she expected him to cleverly maneuver the conversation in the direction of Betty Parnet, so he surprised her. He talked about the weather, and gradually shifted his interest from Miss Johnson to the steak.

His thoughts had turned to Betty Parnet and the puzzle of her relationship with Nick Falcone, and he was startled to hear Miss Johnson pronouncing the opening words of an introduction. "Marilyn, this is—" She turned to him politely. "I don't believe I know your name."

"Ron Webber," he said, gravely studying the newcomer. She had slid into the chair beside him without his noticing.

"Mr. Webber, Miss Andrews."

"Your name sounds familiar," Webber said calmly. Familiar like sixteen-inch headlines.

"Marilyn shared an apartment with Betty Parnet," Miss Johnson said.

Webber turned his attention to Marilyn Andrews. She was a blond like Betty Parnet, only more so. She was much smaller— she couldn't have been more than five feet two—and her pert, dimpled face should have been radiantly lovely. But her mouth had a forlorn droop and there was a freshly-scrubbed look about her, which was explained by the way she kept dabbing her handkerchief at her reddened eyes. Beneath the heavy shadow of tragedy her eyes were deeply blue. She wore a blue necklace, and a neat print dress, with small blue flowers on white. Webber wondered what she would look like when she smiled.

"I can't get over it," she said.

"It doesn't do any good to cry about it," Miss Johnson said reproachfully.

Webber said to Marilyn, "I understand that you work for Ronson and Wilcox, too." He wondered why he hadn't seen her that morning.

"I do," she said.

"He's some kind of an investigator," Miss Johnson said. "He was asking questions about Betty."

Marilyn dabbed again with her handkerchief. "She was so proud about getting that car, too."

"Let's not talk about it," Miss Johnson said firmly.

Webber turned sideways, and cut her out of the conversation. "I talked to Mrs. Warren this morning. She said that Betty had just bought the car."

"Yes. She bought it yesterday. I went over to Hunterton last night to see my parents. My mother's been sick. Betty called me at the office and wanted to drive me over, but she wasn't exactly sure about the time the man would bring the car, so I caught a bus up town and went right from work. Then I missed the bus this morning, and it was ten when I got back, so I went right to the office from the bus station, and that was the first I heard about it." She dabbed with her handkerchief again.

"I don't suppose you know who she bought the car from," Webber said.

Marilyn turned. "What was the man's name?"

Miss Johnson shook her head. "I don't know anything about it."

"Martin, I think. He's one of Mr. Ronson's clients. Or maybe it's Mr. Wilcox. Anyway Betty was crazy about getting a car, and she's been talking about it with everyone for a long time, so

Mr. Martin said he would find one for her."

"It couldn't have been Mr. Martin," Ruth Johnson said. "He's in the real estate business."

"I think it was Martin—or some name like Martin. I don't really know who he is. I just remember Betty mentioning the name. She couldn't afford a car, but this was supposed to be such a good buy that she couldn't refuse it. Somebody couldn't keep up the payments, and she got it by paying the balance."

"Have you told the police about this?"

They both stared at him. "Why on earth would the police want to know about it?" Miss Johnson asked.

"I haven't talked to anyone," Marilyn said. "I haven't even been back to the apartment."

"The police have to check on everything," Webber said. "There may be some complication about the car's ownership, or the insurance. Here." He scribbled a note to Bob Hendricks on the back of one of his cards. "As soon as you've finished eating, you take this to police headquarters. Ask for Mr. Hendricks. Tell him, or somebody there, everything that you know about this. I'll guarantee that they'll be interested."

"If you really think it's important—" She tucked the card into her purse.

Miss Johnson pushed back her chair, and reached for her check. Webber got his hand on it first. "No dessert?" he asked. "How about more coffee?"

"I have to hurry back. We're shorthanded today. One of the girls is sick, and with Betty—that isn't necessary. Let me have it, please."

"I'll put it on my expense account," Webber said. He didn't have an expense account, but it seemed the proper thing for him to do. She shrugged, thanked him and walked away.

"Would you mind talking about Betty?" Webber said to Marilyn.

"I guess not."

"Did she have any boyfriends?"

She shook her head. "No. Lots of fellows asked for dates,

but she wouldn't go out with them. Her mother married rather young, and had a pretty bad time of it, I guess. Betty said she wouldn't make the same mistake. She thought someday she'd get married and have a family, but she wanted to enjoy herself for a while without any romantic complications."

"Did she ever mention a man named Falcone?"

"I've heard that name, but I don't think Betty mentioned it. Could he be one of the clients?"

"It's possible," Webber said. Nick Falcone would have the best lawyer available, and it would explain how Betty Parnet happened to meet him."

Webber pursued his questioning gently but persistently. Betty Parnet had not mentioned any intention of buying insurance. An agent had been trying to sell policies to both of them, but he wanted them to take big policies instead of the small ones they thought they needed, so they hadn't bought. Betty wouldn't have bought any kind of a policy without telling Marilyn about it. Besides, she was saving her money for the car.

Webber consulted his notebook. He was interested in establishing Betty Parnet's exact whereabouts at the times she was supposed to have been buying an insurance policy and seeing the insurance company's doctors. Marilyn Andrews could not tell him about Betty's Saturday activity, because she hadn't worked that day. But she stated flatly that Betty had not left the office on Monday morning, not even for coffee.

"We never go out for coffee," she said. "Mr. Ronson has it sent up, and we have it in the library. Betty didn't even leave the office at noon on Monday. We took our lunches, and ate in the library. Sally went down and brought up coffee and ice cream sundaes for us."

"You're a good witness, Marilyn."

A wan suggestion of a smile touched her face. "Why do you ask all these questions?"

Figuring it would do no harm, Webber told her about the insurance application.

"No," she said. She shook her head emphatically. "I know it

wasn't Betty. Why would anyone try to do that?"

"We don't know. Who would be able to tell me the exact times she was in the office on Saturday?"

"I don't know. A couple of the other girls worked. I could ask."

Webber consulted his notebook again. "And Monday evening—you and Betty ate with some friends and went to a movie. Is that right?"

"Yes. Five of us spent the evening together. We ate here. The food is usually good, but it's too expensive for us to come very often."

Webber captured Marilyn's check as they finished eating, and offered to accompany her to police headquarters.

"Will it take long?" she asked.

"It might take a while. They'll have quite a few questions for you. I'm surprised they haven't looked you up before now."

"Then I'd better get back to the office first, and tell them where I'm going."

Webber paid the three checks, and walked over to collect his car. He drove north, and turned onto Front Street three blocks west of the National Credit Company office, hoping wistfully that fate would treat him to a convenient parking place. Fate almost passed him by, and then relented at the last minute. At the beginning of the fourth block a car was just pulling out from the curb. Webber slammed on his brakes, and hummed a fervent Hosanna as he swung into the empty space. He grabbed the door handle with his left hand and his briefcase with his right hand, and hesitated.

The intersection behind him was clear, but he reminded himself that lightning had struck Frank Milford out of a clear sky. He had no doubt that the Old Man was right—whoever was playing this game wasn't after blue ribbons.

He slid across the front seat, opened the right-hand door, and stepped out onto the sidewalk. As he turned to pick up his briefcase, he saw a blue sedan. It was drifting by slowly. The right front window was rolled down. A hand was steadying a

.45 automatic on the car door.

As Webber threw himself to the sidewalk the first shot snapped over his head and struck a store window behind him. There were other shots, rifling claps of sound spewing up out of the swirl of traffic noises as the gunman realized what Webber had done and tried to get at him.

Finally there was the straining whine of a sustained acceleration, and the sedan was gone.

CHAPTER SIX

Webber struggled to a sitting position. A strange face was peering down at him. It was an extremely plump face, with thick brows that fluttered excitedly and a small mouth that opened and closed without saying anything. For some reason the effect seemed ridiculously comic, and Webber laughed.

He got to his feet and glanced nervously down the street. The blue sedan had vanished. He brushed himself off, and found the strange face still regarding him intently. This time the mouth produced a voice. "Are you all right?"

Webber did not answer. A crowd had formed out of nowhere, pressing in on him, talking excitedly.

"Are you all right?" the voice said again. "I'm a doctor."

"I'll let you know as soon as I stop shaking," Webber said.

The voice laughed, and when the doctor had assured himself that Webber was unharmed, the laugh lost itself in the crowd. A fat man pushed through to Webber and thrust a piece of paper at him. "I saw the whole thing. That's the license number."

Webber thanked him, and congratulated him on his eyesight. He wrote down his name, and managed to pick another eye witness out of the crowd. At the front of his car several men were discussing the damage in awed tones. One slug had scarred the windshield. Two more had caught the radiator, and another the right front tire. Over by the building, a smaller crowd had gathered. The little Italian haberdasher was performing mournful gyrations in front of his pocked plate glass window. A police car rounded the corner, siren and brakes screaming.

Webber knew the officers. He gave them a description of the car, introduced them to his two eyewitnesses, and told them where they could find him. He climbed the stairs to the National Credit Company office, and found Boyd looking down at the crowd from the front window.

"What happened?" he asked.

"Someone took a few shots at me."

Webber telephoned a garage, arranged to have his car towed away and a substitute car supplied while repairs were being made. He telephoned his automobile insurance agent, and broke the bad news gently. Boyd was still standing at the window when he hung up.

"How did they happen to miss you?" he asked, dryly.

"If I'd gotten out of my car on the street side, they wouldn't have missed."

"I don't like this."

"I didn't exactly enjoy it myself."

"Do you think it's wise to go ahead?"

"It doesn't make sense," Webber said. "None of it makes sense. The information is there waiting for anyone who'll go out and ask a few questions. The police already have anything I've turned up, or they will have it whenever they get around to going after it."

"The gunman seems to differ with you on that. The police don't agree with you, either. Your dad telephoned this morning. He told me to keep my amateurs out of this."

"I hope you straightened him out."

"I did. But I'm not sure that he wasn't right."

One of the officers came in. Webber gave him a statement, and referred him to Bob Hendricks for background. He followed the officer back to the sidewalk, watched the wrecker tow his car away, and got the substitute car into the same parking place. It was a good parking place, and he saw no reason for wasting it.

He went back to the office and sat down at his desk. The reaction hit him hard. He lit a cigarette, held it at arm's length, and tried to keep his hand from shaking. "A good investigator," he told himself, "would carry on as if nothing had happened." A good investigator. A Frank Milford. Frank would have popped up from behind a fender and thumbed his nose at the gunman between shots.

Doris Kline, Boyd's secretary, was regarding him fixedly from the other side of the room. Her plump face seemed pale. Webber grinned at her, and the smile he got in return was wispy and unnatural.

"Any requisitions come in by special messenger?" he asked.

She sighed. "I'll never hear the end of that. What would you have done with it?"

"Has it ever happened before?"

"Not while I've worked here, and that's seven years. I suppose I should have told Mr. Boyd, but I knew he'd have the report the next day, and it didn't seem like anything to make a fuss about. It was just another requisition. How could I know that it was a phony?"

"He didn't get it the next day, though," Webber said thoughtfully.

"No. Mr. Greenway didn't finish it before we left."

"If it ever happens again, I think I'd check with the insurance company's local office."

"I certainly will," she said fervently. "I'll check with them, and with Mr. Boyd, and get an okay from the District Attorney."

Webber's hand had stopped shaking. "Work," he said, and went to the files.

He pulled the file on William J. Howard. It was ten years old, but Grade A all the way. Howard needed thirty-five thousand dollars like Webber needed a new shoe lace. There was no file on Martin.

The real estate man was not Webber's problem, but he called the Chamber of Commerce and the clerk told him Martin was originally from the west coast by way of a small upstate community, and that he had located in Carter City four years before. Webber let it go at that. Martin was a police problem, not connected with the insurance application in any way that

Webber could see. He started typing up his notes, and he was still at it half an hour later, when Boyd opened the door of his private office and beckoned to him.

"Supposing we talk about it," Boyd said.

Webber moved a chair up to Boyd's desk, and spread out his notes. He took another glance at Greenway's report before he began, and found himself riveted by a fact that had not penetrated his consciousness before. "Before she went to work for Ronson and Wilcox, Betty Parnet worked for the city," he said. "I wonder if Jim Huss knew her."

Boyd scowled. "Who is Jim Huss?"

"City engineer."

"What does he have to do with it?"

"Maybe nothing," Webber said. "It's something for Hendricks to look into, I suppose. Still—I wonder what department she worked in. Ralph just says she worked for the city and was highly thought of."

"Look into it if you think it's important."

"It probably isn't, from our point of view. I'll give it to Hendricks. Well, what I have shapes up like this. Betty Parnet was physically and morally qualified to buy all the insurance she could afford. Her income didn't justify the purchase of a thirty-five thousand dollar policy, and if she had been buying it herself, she wouldn't have been able to pay for it. If her uncle had been buying it for her, as this phony Betty Parnet told Ralph, she could have qualified for any amount. I turned up some derogatory information from a former landlady of hers, but it's peculiar, and information from other sources pretty well cancels it out. I doubt if it's worth considering."

"What about the application?"

"I break it down like this. First step—Jones writes the application on Saturday morning in the Carter Restaurant. I've found a waitress who knew Betty Parnet by sight, and who also saw Jones writing up the application. She says that the girl buying the insurance was not Betty Parnet, but another girl who has eaten in the restaurant before. Jones says that the girl who bought the insurance was not Betty Parnet. To round that off, Betty Parnet was working Saturday, and I should be able to find someone who can place her elsewhere at the same time that Jones wrote the application."

Boyd nodded, and went to work on his pipe. "Go on."

"The next steps are the medical examinations, Saturday afternoon and Monday morning. I should be able to place Betty Parnet somewhere else on Saturday afternoon, and I already have a witness who states that she did not leave her place of employment on Monday morning. Then we have the statements of both doctors to the effect that the girl they examined was not Betty Parnet."

"Then we have Greenway's inspection. He states that the girl he interviewed was not Betty Parnet. I have one witness, and can probably find three more, to testify that Betty Parnet was eating dinner up town at the same time that Greenway was interviewing an unknown girl out on Sunset Boulevard. I also have a statement from a neighbor to the effect that a strange girl who claimed to be waiting for Betty Parnet was sitting on the porch about the time that Greenway got there, and disappeared later—presumably after talking with Greenway. The neighbor didn't actually see them talking, but that isn't critical."

"There are assorted odds and ends to round it out, one of them being Frank's notes to the effect that she denied applying for the insurance, and wouldn't have named her uncle as a beneficiary if she had applied."

"Star Mutual couldn't ask for much more," Boyd said. "The only thing lacking is a notarized statement by Betty Parnet to the effect that she didn't apply for the insurance, and we'd have had that if she hadn't been killed. How much longer do you expect to take?"

"Do I pull in all these loose ends, or just let it stand the way it is?"

"Let's not have any loose ends."

"If I'm lucky I'll finish by noon tomorrow. I've been lucky so far."

"I'd say you've been very lucky, and I'm not referring to the investigation. When is Frank's funeral?"

"Friday afternoon. One o'clock."

"We'll close the office Friday afternoon. Let me know if I can help with anything."

Webber pounded his forehead gently. "I still have a few things to look after. I was going to order flowers, and—"

"Let Doris do it. Women understand these things."

"Thanks, I will."

He finished typing up his notes, and put one copy in the file and a carbon in his desk. He walked over to the window. The sky had clouded up, and if rain were not imminent the atmosphere was putting on a convincing bluff. He studied the clouds, and scowled. Rain was bad for an investigator. It was hard to stand with water dripping down your neck and ask questions in a dignified manner.

Doris looked at him inquiringly as he turned away. "Work," he said, and started for the door.

Bob Hendricks was getting out of a patrol car as Webber reached the sidewalk. Hendricks waved the car on its way, and hurried toward him. "You all right, kid?"

"I stopped being a kid eight years ago," Webber said.

"I guess you're all right. Where can we talk? Your office?"

"I could use some coffee."

Half a block down the street they entered a small café, and found a vacant booth. Webber ordered two cups of coffee, and as soon as the girl had gone, Hendricks leaned across the table and pointed a finger.

"Give. What have you got that made them want to kill you?"

"Nothing."

Hendricks eyed him dubiously. "There has to be something."

"No. I've just talked to people that were obviously connected with the case, and picked up a little background information from neighbors and the like. Anyone can have what I have by going over the same ground." He smiled. "Even a police detective. It's there for the taking."

"I can't believe that. You must have something. They wouldn't try to kill you just because you were making inquiries."

"I've typed up everything I have. There's a copy in the files. Drop in at the office any time, and Doris will let you read it."

"I'll do that," Hendricks said. The waitress brought their coffee. Hendricks got out a handkerchief and mopped his face. "We've hardly gotten our teeth into these murders, and now we have another one on our hands. I can't remember the last time Carter City had two separate homicide investigations going on at once, let alone three."

"Anyone I know?"

"I doubt it. Some dame got herself shot. I hope it isn't as confounded involved as this Parnet thing."

"Have you happened on the fact that Betty Parnet used to date Nick Falcone?"

Hendricks blinked. "You're kidding."

"Fact."

"That would explain Pronk's little inquiry—Big Nick wanting to know who bumped her off. If it's anything more than that, where would it leave your insurance application?"

"I don't know. Then there's the fact that she used to work for the city."

"So?"

"I was wondering if she worked in the engineer's office."

"Water department, I think. But that's next door to the engineer's office. You realize, don't you that you're not making this thing any less complicated?"

"Have you turned up anything on this Martin character?"

"Martin? Who's he?"

"Didn't you talk with the Andrews girl?"

Hendricks consulted his notebook. "Andrews? Marilyn Andrews? That's the girl that was sharing the apartment with Parnet. She's on my list, but I haven't seen her yet."

"I met her this noon. She has some good information. She thinks she knows the name of the man who was supposed to sell Betty Parnet a car yesterday. I gave her a note to you, and told her to get down to headquarters as soon as she could."

"I've been out most of the afternoon. This other murder scrambled things. The man's name was Martin?"

"She said Martin or something like Martin. There's a Bertram Martin among the Ronson and Wilcox clients. Real estate agent—the Chamber of Commerce says he comes originally from the west coast."

Hendricks emptied his coffee cup. "Excuse me," he said. He strode to the far end of the room, and bent over a pay telephone.

"I'm having a check made on Martin," he said, when he returned. "The girl didn't show. She works for Ronson and Wilcox, doesn't she?"

Webber nodded.

"Suppose you come along. I'll let you introduce me."

Webber drove his rented car. He got in on the right side, and slid across the front seat. Hendricks got in after him, and asked no questions.

There were no parking places in the vicinity of the National Bank building. Webber circled the block once, and then Hendricks directed him into a loading zone, and flashed his credentials at the man who ran out to protest.

Ruth Johnson looked up from the switchboard as they entered the law office, her smile already in place. Her eyes widened when she saw Webber, and the smile dissolved slowly around its edges. It kept dissolving as Hendricks introduced himself. When she turned back to Webber her mouth was a sticky red line.

"We'd like to talk with Marilyn Andrews," Webber said.

"She went to the police station. She hasn't come back yet."

Webber looked blankly at Hendricks.

"Get police headquarters," Hendricks snapped, and as she turned to the switchboard, he said, "Just a moment. How long ago did she leave?"

"I don't know exactly," she said. "It couldn't have been too long after one."

"What time was it when you saw her?" Hendricks asked

Webber.

"It was during the noon hour. We left the restaurant a little after twelve-thirty, and she said she was coming back here, and then she'd go over to headquarters."

"Did she come back here?" Hendricks asked.

"Yes," Ruth Johnson said. "It was—well, not too long after I got back myself. Before one o'clock, I think, though I wasn't paying much attention to the clock. Then a little later she left, and said she was going to the police station."

"Would you check, please and find out if anyone knows anything about this."

There was no politeness in his voice. It was a blunt command, and though his face was expressionless, Webber sensed the frustration he felt.

Ruth Johnson made a panicky exit, and a moment later a big, portly, white-haired man came charging out of a private office and kicked over a wastebasket as he crossed the room. He wore no coat or tie. His shirt sleeves were half rolled up, and his plaid suspenders curved tautly over his protruding stomach. He faced Hendricks with a deepening red face and clenched fists.

From somewhere in the background, Ruth Johnson said meekly, "This is Mr. Wilcox."

"Now see here!" Wilcox raised one fist and shook it under Hendricks's nose. "I don't like my employees being bothered while they're working."

"I suppose you've heard what happened to one of your employees, Betty Parnet," Hendricks said coldly.

"I can assure you, young man, that her employment here had nothing to do with an automobile accident."

"You'll find in the papers tonight that she didn't have an accident. She was murdered. If we don't find Marilyn Andrews quickly, you may be reading the same thing about her tomorrow morning."

Wilcox pivoted to glance about the office. "Where's Marilyn?"

"I don't know," Ruth Johnson said. "She said she was going—"

"Sally!" Wilcox snapped.

A dark-haired girl jumped nervously. "Yes Mr. Wilcox?"

"Have you seen Marilyn?"

"She came back from lunch early, and talked to Mr. Ronson. I think she typed something for him, and then he sent her on an errand. I haven't seen her since then."

"See if Ed is busy," Wilcox said. Ruth Johnson hurried away. "You say Betty was murdered?"

"She was," Hendricks said levelly.

"Nonsense. You police have so little to do you have to make a murder out of a simple automobile accident. Why, there wasn't even another car involved, was there?"

They turned as a slim, meticulously-dressed man walked toward them. He was completely bald, and his face was a grotesque caricature, with an overly-large nose and a hideous, pock-marked complexion. His small, alert eyes captured the attention and held it. His manner and smile were friendly. He stopped beside them, hands on his hips, and said good-naturedly, "What's the problem, gentlemen?"

"Police," Wilcox said. "Maybe you can tell them what they want to know. Dratted waste of time, I say." He stomped away, paused to straighten the overturned wastebasket, and disappeared into his office with a decisive bang of the door.

"We're looking for Marilyn Andrews," Hendricks was saying.

Ronson glanced toward an unoccupied desk. "Isn't she back yet, Ruth?"

Ruth Johnson shook her head.

"Well—then you know more about it than I do. She left here to go to police headquarters."

"Did you see her before she left?" Hendricks asked.

"Yes. She came in about a quarter to one. I was just getting ready to go to lunch. She said she wanted to tell the police something about Betty, and I asked her to type a couple of letters before she left, and drop them off at the Post Office. I wanted them to make the two o'clock plane. I haven't seen her since."

"Did she tell you why she wanted to talk to us?"

"No."

"You didn't ask her?"

Ronson seemed mildly surprised. "She was living with Betty Parnet. I didn't think it unusual that the police would want to talk to her, considering what happened.

"You asked her to mail some letters. May I have the addresses that were on those letters?"

Ronson frowned. "I'm always happy to cooperate with the police, but usually—oh well." He called Sally over, and gave her whispered instructions. She went to the files, and from there to her desk. She brought Ronson a piece of paper with two addresses typed on it, and he handed it to Hendricks.

"The contents of the letters are confidential. I trust that this will be sufficient."

"It will."

"I don't quite understand what you're getting at, but if you think you do—"

"I think I do. Here's my card. If Marilyn Andrews comes back here, I'd like to know about it. Immediately. I'd say the chances are about a thousand to one against it, but if she does I'd like to know. The addresses are so I can find out whether she disappeared before or after she got as far as the Post Office."

Ronson's hands snapped to his hips. "You mean she didn't go to the police headquarters?"

"As of twenty minutes ago, she hadn't got there."

Ronson grinned broadly, and shook his head. "What a girl won't do to get the afternoon off!"

Hendricks turned away. By the time Webber reached the hallway he was already halfway to the elevator. Webber sprinted after him.

"How well can you describe this Andrews girl?" Hendricks asked over his shoulder.

"Fairly well. She's small—not a lot over five feet. She has a good figure with all the right proportions. She's blonde, but not the flashy kind of blonde. More of a yellow. She has blue eyes, and dimples in both cheeks, and nice-looking teeth. She was wearing a flowered dress, white with blue flowers, and a necklace with some kind of blue stones in it."

In the lobby, Hendricks jumped for a telephone booth, and Webber walked slowly toward the entrance. Outside he found a delivery truck double-parked, a patrol car pulled up behind it, and an excited conference in progress over the presence of his car in the loading zone.

Hendricks appeared before Webber could finish his explanation. He settled the matter with a few sharp words, and the delivery truck pulled ahead to let Webber out.

"Can you drop me off at headquarters?" Hendricks asked.

"Sure. Hop in."

"If you're in a hurry about something, don't bother."

"No hurry. I have an appointment with Howard at four, but I have plenty of time to make that."

Hendricks waved the men in the patrol car about their business, and climbed in beside Webber. "Any word on Marilyn Andrews?" Webber asked him.

"She hasn't showed at headquarters. The desk sergeant wants to know if you got her ring size."

Webber grunted, and took a corner on slightly less than four wheels.

"No offense," Hendricks said. "It's just that it was an unusually detailed description. I hope she's all right. I hope we find her. Do you have a gun?"

"I had one once. I suppose dad still has it. It was registered in his name."

"Since you have some time, stop off at headquarters and I'll loan you one."

"I haven't any use for it," Webber said quietly.

"Nonsense. If you won't keep your nose out of this, you can at least be ready to defend yourself."

"Do you really think they'll try again?"

"Why not?"

"That would make even less sense. I've had time to type up

my notes, and go over the whole thing with you. Even if I'd turned up something important, killing me wouldn't help them if I've already passed the information along."

"You might happen onto something else."

Webber shook his head. "I expect to finish by noon tomorrow, and then you can have your murders all to yourself."

"Thanks." Hendricks said. "I won't tell you what the Old Man said when he heard about that little adventure of yours."

Webber let Hendricks out at Headquarters, and stopped at a drugstore for a fast cup of coffee before he went to see William J. Howard.

The title of consulting engineer suggested rows of blueprints to Webber, and Howard's office surprised him. There was a cubbyhole of an outer office, where a comfortable-looking middle-aged secretary relaxed indolently behind a desk that nearly filled the room. She looked at Webber's card, nodded, and walked over to bang lustily on a door.

"Mr. Webber," she called.

"Send him in," a voice growled.

She jerked her thumb at the door, and returned to her magazine. Webber said to himself, "He certainly is in the business only for the fun of it." He opened the door.

Howard was standing at his desk, shoulders erect, his arms folded. His facial expression reflected the same formidable stiffness. He was a small man, dry and unemotional-looking, with a trim little mustache that was just perceptibly graying. On his desk, uncovered for action was a monstrous electric adding machine.

"Perhaps I can save time for both of us," Howard said. He snapped out his words in a thin, high-pitched voice. "I know nothing of any life insurance application made by my niece, Betty Parnet. I did not know my niece. To the best of my knowledge I have never seen her. I have no intention of claiming benefits under any insurance she owned or may have intended owning. Does that cover the ground sufficiently?"

"No," Webber said, making an effort not to smile. "No it

doesn't." Howard was the type who would consider any problem in adding machine terms. Push the right buttons, read off the total, clear the machine and get on with something else.

"I don't know what else you can ask. I haven't consulted an attorney, but I don't think any insurance company can force me to take money I don't want."

"I can relieve you of concern on that point," Webber said, watching him closely. "No money will be paid on the insurance application made in the name of Betty Parnet."

Howard accepted that as he might have accepted another column of figures. Click. He added it. "Thank you. Then you won't need any information from me. Good afternoon." He sat down.

"I may need a lot of information from you," Webber said. The fact that he was becoming increasingly curious about William J. Howard and his curiosity included points that were not strictly germane to his insurance investigation.

"Would you mind telling me why?" Howard asked.

Webber stated the facts. The application for insurance had been fraudulent. Betty Parnet had been murdered. The insurance company naturally wanted a full investigation of the insurance application and the police were interested in knowing if the insurance application was in any way connected with the murder. And the only person who could benefit from the insurance was the beneficiary named in the application, William J. Howard.

Howard bristled. "Are you trying to involve me in this?"

"You're already involved."

Howard pushed the adding machine aside, got a cigar out of a desk drawer, and trimmed the end deftly. There was a chair at the corner of his desk, but he did not extend an invitation, so Webber remained standing.

"I suppose I am," he said finally, "Since I'm supposed to be the beneficiary. Just what do you want to know?"

"How did Betty Parnet happen to be in Carter City?"

"I don't see what difference that makes. But—all right. Her

mother was my sister. I'd completely lost touch with my family. Left home when I was a kid, you know. Then early last year— January or February—I had a letter from Betty Parnet. I didn't even recognize the name—never knew who my sister married. Through some roundabout way she'd gotten my address. She said her parents were dead, and she was living in a small town where there weren't many opportunities. She'd had secretarial training in high school, and taken some kind of home study course, and she wondered if it would be imposing on me to ask me to help her get a job in Carter City."

He paused to puff on the cigar. "It was a straight-forward letter, and of course that sort of thing is hardly an imposition. If she was ambitious enough to want to work, I'd have been glad to help her. But there were—and are—lots of opportunities here for girls with a little secretarial training. I told her that, and suggested she come down and pick out her own job.

"I don't know when she came, or where she went to work, and the next time I heard from her was late last year. She had an opportunity for a better job with Ronson and Wilcox, and she asked me to give her a recommendation. I've known Jim Wilcox for years. He's been my attorney for years. I called him, and told him the girl was my niece and an orphan, and though I didn't know her personally and couldn't tell him anything about her, I'd consider it a favor if he would give her an opportunity. Assuming, of course that there wasn't anything objectionable about her.

"That was the last time I heard from her or of her. No—once after that Jim told me he'd hired her, and she was working out fine."

"Did she come to see you when she asked for the recommendation?"

"No. Wrote me a letter. I told you I've never laid eyes on her."

"That seems odd. Wilcox is your legal advisor, and she worked in his office for a number of months."

Howard's mouth formed a wry little smile, but his face remained stern.

"I don't need much legal advice these days. Back when I did, I had dinner with Jim and talked it over. I can't remember the last time I was in his office."

"There's the matter of the car Betty Parnet was driving."

"Had it parked out front. I was leaving for New York, and I went out, and it was gone. I reported it to the police, and took a cab to the airport."

"Do you think Betty Parnet stole it?"

The smile touched his face again, but only for an instant. "Frankly no. I had a stern bringing up in a society where nice young girls didn't steal cars, or anything else. Maybe times have changed, or maybe not. That's a police problem."

"If she wanted to steal a car," Webber said, "It would be quite a coincidence that of all the cars in Carter City she happened to take yours."

"I feel the same way about it. But as I said, it's a police problem."

Webber measured him carefully. "You might be interested to know that I have evidence from several sources to the effect that she bought your car."

"I rather hoped that she didn't steal it."

Webber smiled in the general direction of the adding machine. "That still doesn't explain the coincidence. Someone stole your car and sold it, which is easy enough to understand. But of all the people in Carter City who might have bought it, the purchaser turned out to be your niece. Can you explain that?"

"No," Howard said. "I'm happy that I don't have to explain it. Is there anything else?"

"Yes. You are Betty Parnet's only relative in this area. You gave her advice that worked out well for her, and your recommendation helped her to obtain a better job. Why did she tell our investigator on Tuesday morning that you were the last person she would think of making a life insurance beneficiary?"

He deliberately exaggerated the effect, and he got it. Howard winced. "She said that? Well, why not? We'd never met. I was a stranger who'd written her one letter and made one telephone call for her. And—" The smile returned. "—she no doubt had close friends who needed the money. I don't.

"Thank you very much," Webber said.

Howard nodded. He was already reaching for the adding machine before Webber got out of the room. The secretary did not look up from her magazine as Webber went by. He walked back to his car slowly, because some puzzling impressions were misbehaving in his mind, and he needed to think.

If William J. Howard ever wanted to commit murder, he would be unlikely to use an automobile. He would do it by short-circuiting an adding machine. But suppose he jobbed out his dirty work?

Obviously the events leading up to the deaths of Betty Parnet and Frank Milford were a long time in the making, and a number of people were involved. Someone had masterminded it. Howard?

But Howard would not point attention at himself by having his niece die in his own car. On the surface there was nothing illogical about him being the beneficiary of the insurance policy. Of course Betty Parnet had told Frank Milford that she wouldn't name her uncle as her beneficiary, but whoever planned this thing couldn't know that would happen. So the beneficiary part of it was logical enough, but where did the car fit in?

However it fit, Webber was convinced of one thing. Howard was in. He was connected in some way. He had to be. Taken by itself, either the beneficiary business or the stolen car might be coincidence. Taken together, no.

He sat in his car and smoked a cigarette, and finally he decided that he'd done his day's work, and that he could think better at home. He drove away, and before he had traveled a block he knew he was being followed.

He was already familiar with the technique. It was high-class, and this time there was a difference. Two differences. One was the brown car. The other was the uncanny knowledge of Carter City that the driver had picked up since morning.

Webber tried a simple trick. He opened up a block lead, and

made a quick turn into an ally that had three exits. He emerged two blocks away, made his turn, and far up the street the brown car pulled out of a driveway and followed him.

"What d'ya know!" Webber exclaimed.

There were times when he would have enjoyed matching wits with that driver, but he was dead tired, and he'd used up the last of his patience on William J. Howard. He made another turn, and headed up a side street. He reached the main gate of the Carter City Manufacturing Company just in time to become entangled in the exodus of the day shift. An officer was directing traffic at the intersection. Webber recognized him, and grinned.

He opened his car door and looked back. The brown car was in line behind him. There were two men in the front seat. Webber slammed his door, and waited.

Eventually the officer cut off the flow from the plant parking lot, and waved the cross traffic through. Webber pulled up beside him.

"Do me a favor, Mike."

"Sure, Ronny."

"I'm being tailed. It's the fourth car back—the brown car. Cut him off, and give me a few minutes."

Webber let out the clutch, and shot away. When he looked back the plant traffic was moving again, and the brown car was no longer following.

He drove directly home, circled the block twice and parked over on the next street. The telephone was ringing in his apartment as he came up the stairs. He got the door open and raced across the room, but the ringing had stopped. From Frank Milford's desk the little angel furnished an appropriate gesture.

The telephone rang again just as he was climbing out of the shower. He left a moist path between the bathroom and telephone, and Bob Hendricks's voice exploded at him.

'I called Howard," he said, "and he said you'd left. Your office said you weren't expected back. And you weren't home. Where the hell were you?"

"I had a tail to shake on my way home. It must have been you that hung up just as I got to the phone."

"What sort of tail?"

"A good one. Brown car—I didn't let him get very close."

"Look. After you left I remembered you telling me you'd typed up your notes, and I could read them at the office. So I went over and read them. Do you remember the murder I was telling you about? The dame that got shot?"

"I remember."

"Well, you asked if it was anyone you knew and I said no. I was wrong. Are you going to be home for a while?"

"Sure. I'll be here."

"I'll be right over."

"Who was it that got murdered?"

"An old dame. Betty Parnet's former landlady. Mrs. Charlotte Lamont."

CHAPTER SEVEN

Webber, wearing only a bathrobe, sat on the sofa and stared fixedly at the carpet. The pattern of dull red on brown had been under his feet for nearly a year and a half, but never before had the red suggested blood to him.

Hendricks paced back and forth, carrying an ash tray and forgetting to use it. They both started when the telephone rang. Hendricks snatched at it, listened briefly, and slammed it down.

"That settles it," he said. "The same gun that made your life interesting this afternoon killed the old woman."

"I might just as well have shot her myself," Webber said. "I could have given that car the slip, but I let it follow me."

"Forget it. Obviously she knew too much, and you can't blame yourself for that. Question is what did she know?"

"She connected Betty Parnet with Nick Falcone."

Hendricks waved the ash tray gloomily. "In that case, where does Marilyn Andrews fit in? This thing has two handles to it, and I don't like either of them."

He turned a chair backwards and straddled facing Webber. "Take the Marilyn Andrews handle. You talk to her in a restaurant, and she has some interesting information, and you encourage her to go to the police. Result: she disappears, and someone tries to eliminate you. If they'd succeeded, we wouldn't have known about the guy Martin."

"Ruth Johnson could have told you."

"She could have, but would she? Maybe yes, maybe no. I had her tabbed as the one who put the finger on Andrews and you."

"We don't know who else Marilyn may have talked with either at the office or outside. In fact, we don't know who Johnson may have talked with, or who may have overheard us at the restaurant."

"Agreed, but I was going to pull Johnson in for some stiff questioning, just on general principles. Then Lamont gets murdered and you toss this Falcone thing at me.

"So we have another handle to work on. You're tailed to Lamont's house. She knows something, maybe she tells you and maybe she doesn't but they don't take chances. You leave Mrs. Lamont shortly after eleven thirty, and she's murdered between twelve and one, after you shake your tail. Then the murderers figure you'll go back to the National Credit office sooner or later, so they wait for you. If they'd been successful you wouldn't have written your report, and we wouldn't have known about the Falcone-Parnet business. We might not have connected Mrs. Lamont's murder with the Parnet murder.

"The question is, how does the Andrews disappearance fit in with this Falcone thing, or what's the connection between Falcone and Martin? If you tell me they're obviously related I'll kick you in the teeth. I've been taking them apart and putting them together again for an hour, and I just can't make them fit."

"There's one common denominator. Betty Parnet."

"Sure. All three of them lived in Carter City, too. If Andrews is dead, as I suspect, then all three of them have that in common. There are lots of common denominators."

"It wouldn't hurt to ask Nick Falcone a few questions."

"Oh, we'll do that—when and if we find him. But of all the charges I never expect to hang on Big Nick, a murder rap is the last one. Would it surprise you if I told you Big Nick is one of the most responsible and law abiding citizens in Carter City?"

"It seems to me I've heard otherwise."

"You hear a lot about Big Nick, but none of it has ever been proven. Why? Because there isn't anything to prove. This has puzzled me for years. Carter City is the cleanest city of its size in the country. It'll stay that way as long as your dad is Chief of Police. Still, we have the notorious Big Nick Falcone in residence. We have a known racketeer, but no racketeering. We have a known Vice Lord, but no organized vice. No, I'm not kidding. Big Nick has never been arrested, let alone convicted of anything. We harass his known henchmen all the time, but we've never found any evidence worth showing in court. There just isn't any around to collect."

"He's slick" Webber said. "While you dash around harassing his known henchmen, his unknown henchmen clean up."

"It could be," Hendricks mused. "He must get his money somewhere. After all the work we've done trying to tag him with a lousy gambling charge, it'd be laughable if we put him away for murder."

"Has anything else turned up?"

"We lifted some prints from Howard's car. We're waiting for a report, but I'm not hopeful. Anyone in Carter City could have touched that car when it was parked somewhere. We found the blue sedan. Another stolen car, with license plates courtesy of the thief. They seem to have an unlimited supply of plates."

"They saved them up for this."

"It looks that way. The Old Man is behaving the quietest I've seen him since one day when he tried to question Prof Pronk by himself. He practically ordered you off the case, and you respond by turning up the only good leads that we've had."

"Accidently."

"We'd have gotten to Andrews and Lamont, but we weren't in any hurry about either of them. That's the trouble with a case like this. There are a lot of angles, and we should cover all of them at once, and we just haven't got enough men to do it."

"The telephone rang, and Hendricks grabbed it. "Just a moment, please," he said, and hissed at Webber, "Female."

"I don't know any," Webber said. "Wrong number?" He took the phone.

"Mr. Webber?"

"Yes," Webber said, trying to place the voice.

"This is Ruth Johnson. I saw you today at Ronson and

Wilcox's. And at the Carter Restaurant. Do you remember me?

"Of course."

"I've been thinking—and I'd like to talk with you. Could we have dinner together? I could fix something here."

His first reaction was defensive. "I'm sorry. I'm occupied right now. And besides—" The lie slipped out easily. "—I've already eaten."

"Oh," she said. She sounded disappointed. "Well, could you come over later?"

"What was it you want to talk to me about?"

"I'd rather not discuss it on the telephone. It may not be important, of course, but I thought—"

She let the sentence trail away. Webber's thoughts raced in circles. He was physically exhausted, and ready to collapse into bed. On the other hand, it was just possible that she might have something.

"Perhaps I could see you later," he said. "Seven-thirty or -eight?"

"Whenever it's convenient. I'll be here."

"Let's say eight, then. Where do you live?"

"387 Baker. Apartment four. I'll be expecting you."

Webber hung up. "Ruth Johnson. She wants to talk to me about something that may not be important."

Hendricks swore. "I should have pulled her in for questioning. Why is it that people are willing to cooperate with everyone but the police?"

"Why don't you ask people? I cooperate with the police. I'm dog tired, and I'd like to go to bed and sleep twelve hours, but I'm doing this just as a favor to you because you lack personal charm and can't get along with the ladies."

"It can't be your caveman physique that does it. Maybe if I had your pretty face, and your curly hair and long eyelashes—"

"Do you have anything else on your mind? Because if you don't I'm going to get a little rest before I start this next great adventure."

"What's the girl's address?"

"387 Baker. Apartment four."

"All right. Go winging off to your rendezvous, but don't look behind you as you go in the door, because I'm going to have a couple of men there just to see that you get from your car up to the house and back again without being shot. Don't argue. They won't interfere in any way unless Johnson keeps men under her bed, and in that case you can tip them off by throwing something through a window. And they'll stay there after you leave and see that nothing happens to Johnson. One woman you talked to today was kidnapped, and another murdered, and the record speaks for itself."

"Do you have anything at all on Marilyn Andrews?"

"Nothing at all."

Hendricks walked over to the door, looked back with a grin and announced, "This Johnson girl really isn't your type. For one thing, she's too tall for you. But have fun."

The rasping tone of the alarm clock shattered Webber's repose at a quarter after seven. He sat up and hit the alarm button savagely, and then was surprised that he did not feel tired. Fifteen minutes later, having dressed, enjoyed the miracle of instant coffee along with a sandwich, and convinced himself that he didn't need a shave, he knocked on his landlady's door.

Mrs. Mahoney was making doughnuts. She hurried him into the kitchen, put a hot doughnut in his hand, and stepped back to beam at him. Webber bit the doughnut, and pronounced it excellent. "All you need to do," he said, "is touch up that grey hair and get fitted for a new corset, and you'll make some young man a fine wife."

"Get out with you!"

"Would you mind if I went out the back way?"

She gave him a motherly smile. "You go right ahead."

She followed him through the apartment and down the short flight of steps to the rear door. He stood in the doorway, looking through the dusk at the garage, and the alley beyond.

Turning to thank her, he saw that her smile had vanished.

She said hesitantly, "Mr. Webber, the paper tonight said Mr. Milford was murdered."

"I suppose you'd have to call it that," Webber said.

"You think—you think maybe they're after you, too?"

Webber pushed the screen door open. "I certainly hope not. Many thanks."

Her low exclamation floated after him as he hurried down the gravel path toward the garage. He rounded the garage, and move stealthily, almost guiltily, through the yard of a house on the next street. He stood for a moment on the sidewalk, studying the cars that lined both sides of the street. There were no suspicious cars. A newsboy was making his collection rounds, whistling cheerfully as he moved from house to house. A light breeze stirred the trees gently. There were sounds of children playing, of a radio sending forth hot music, of a good natured family argument. It was a world apart from crime and violence.

Webber started for his car, and drove away. The rows of cars remained stationary and lifeless. He circled the block, and stopped twice to check the traffic behind him. Satisfied, he drove through to Lake Street, and headed across town.

The Baker Street houses were newer than those of the Sunset Boulevard area. They were also smaller, and better cared for. The rent would be higher—but perhaps a receptionist-switchboard operator was paid more than a mere office girl.

387 Baker had been remodeled into an apartment building, with two apartments on each floor. Number four was on the second floor front, and Webber climbed the stairway after ringing the bell and getting no response. Ruth Johnson was waiting for him at the top.

"I'm glad you came up," she said. "I decided to change, and you caught me in the act."

She had exchanged the sternly-tailored suit she had worn earlier that day for a light yellow dress of some kind of knit material. With her long black hair the effect was almost pleasing. She had used her cosmetics somewhat less lavishly, and there seemed to be a softer, almost domestic air about her.

"This way," she said, and led him into her apartment.

The furnishings were neat and definitely not shabby, though some of them showed signs of wear. He had time for a quick look around, and because she did not offer him a chair he faced her in the center of the room and waited.

She smiled. "As I said, you caught me at an embarrassing moment. I'm having button trouble. Would you mind giving me a hand?"

She backed towards him, and he forced his clumsy masculine fingers to close the gap in the back of her dress. He made no comment because he was stricken speechless. He turned away quickly when he had finished, and retreated to the sofa on the far side of the room.

She seated herself in an overstuffed chair opposite him, calmly crossed her legs, and took a cigarette from the table beside her. "Will you have one?" she said.

"No thank you, he said. But he crossed the room and held his lighter for her.

He returned to the sofa, and waited for something to happen. She seemed to be studying the print of a very ordinary landscape on the wall behind hem, and she shot an occasional oblique glance in his direction and looked away quickly without meeting his eyes. The silence was becoming embarrassing.

"Do you live by yourself?" he asked.

She told him she did, and added quickly, "It isn't lonely. Not at all. I have friends dropping in all the time. It may not look like much, but this apartment is the nicest place I've ever had to live in my life."

There was another awkward silence. For the want of something to do, Webber lit a cigarette, and got up and found an ash tray for himself. He sat down again, and looked at the clock. It had been a long seven minutes.

"What was it you wanted to see me about?" he said.

"In the restaurant this noon, Marilyn said something about Mr. Martin selling Betty that car. But it wasn't Mr. Martin. I didn't think so then, and now I'm sure of it."

"Someone else wasn't so sure."

"Why do you say that?"

"Marilyn didn't disappear by accident. Someone thought she knew too much."

"She couldn't know any more than a lot of other people know," she said earnestly. "Everyone in the office knew about Betty buying that car. And even if they didn't, you and I know because we were talking about it.

"True," Webber said. "Early this afternoon someone tried to shoot me. You might have been in danger yourself, if you hadn't gone directly back to the office."

She uncrossed her legs, and leaned forward, "Do you think we're still in danger?"

"No."

"But why not?"

"I've already told the police what Marilyn told us. Even the most ruthless criminal knows that there isn't much point in silencing a person who has already talked."

"I never realized," she said. Her voice was a little more than an awed whisper. "I never even suspected. I would have been scared stiff."

"Then it's best that you didn't know."

She lurched to her feet. "Would you like a drink?"

"No thank you."

"Won't you *please* have a drink with me? I'd feel peculiar, drinking by myself."

He shrugged. "All right."

She swished away toward the kitchen, and came back carrying two tall goblets. The red liquid shimmered oddly in the yellow light cast by the floor lamp. She handed one goblet to him, and stood over him, raising hers.

"To—" She hesitated. "To what? Anything in particular?"

"We might drink the very worst of health to Betty Parnet's murderers."

She shuddered, and hunched up her shoulders with her arms pressed closely against her body. "Let's not talk about it," she said, and drained her glass.

Webber took a cautious sip, and swallowed his astonishment. It was wine, and a very bad wine, weak, overly sweet, tasting like a fizzled soda pop gone unaccountably berserk.

She waited while he drank, watching him anxiously. "More?" she said.

"No thank you."

She took the goblets back to the kitchen, and returned and sat down at the opposite end of the sofa. "I wanted to talk to you about Mr. Martin."

"You said it wasn't Martin."

"It wasn't. I've tried to think of his name, but I know it wasn't Martin. It was something like that, but not Martin."

"Do you remember what he looked like?"

"Just vaguely. He was big. A big man. Broad shoulders and a big face and a deep voice. I don't think he was in the office more than two or three times."

"Did you see him talking to Betty Parnet, or hear what he said?"

She shook her head. "I'm on the switchboard, you know, and I don't pay much attention to what goes on behind me. But after he left, once, Betty told me he was going to find her a good car that wouldn't cost much."

Her memory, Webber thought, had undergone a remarkable recovery since noon. "Mr. Ronson or Mr. Wilcox should know who he is, if he came to see one of them on business," he said.

Her voice sank again, to the tremulous, near-whisper. "I did something I shouldn't have."

She looked very frightened, and very ill at ease. In the first minute in her apartment he had her labeled a brazen hussy, and now she was the terrified ingénue. He wondered which role was the natural one, and resisted the impulse to rush forward with a question.

She hesitated, looking away from him. Finally she said, "I went through the files. I thought maybe I could find his name. I think I'd know it if I saw it. But I couldn't find it."

"That seems odd. If he were a client wouldn't his name be in the files?"

She turned quickly, and smiled. "He might not be a client. People come in for all kinds of reasons—selling things, or looking for donations, or running errands. And Mr. Wilcox is in politics, you know, and people come to see him about all sorts of things."

"I see. Well—the police will be asking Mr. Ronson and Mr. Wilcox about it anyway, because of what Marilyn said. They'll probably question everyone in the office."

She looked away from him again. "I felt like a criminal. And it really wasn't necessary."

"You can't say that. You might have found something important, and it would have been necessary."

"That's right. I might have." She smiled. "Would you like another drink?"

"Not right now."

"I suppose you think I'm a terribly odd person."

"We're all odd persons," Webber said. "You aren't any odder than the rest of us."

"You're saying that to be nice."

"No." Suddenly he began to feel very tired. The effects of the nap had worn off, and he was having a hard time keeping his eyes open.

"I'll tell you what you can do," he said. "You can fix me some coffee."

"Of course." She bounded towards the kitchen, and he heard her hurrying through the routine that promised an eventual cup of coffee. "Do you like it strong?" she called.

"Just medium."

She returned wearing a trim little red apron, and took the chair opposite him. "Do the police have any idea who did it—about Betty, I mean."

"I really don't know."

"Oh. You were with that policeman today, and I thought you were helping him."

Webber grinned. "Mr. Hendricks wouldn't like that. He'd tell you I'm not much help. No—I'm just an insurance investigator. I suppose you could say I help the police by passing along information they might be able to use, but they don't give me anything in return. Murders and kidnappings are their business. My business is insurance policies, or insurance applications."

"You mean Mr. Hendricks wouldn't tell you anything about it?"

"If it concerned my investigation, he probably would. But he wouldn't go out of his way to tell me things that are really none of my business. What I know about Betty Parnet's murder is just about what you read in the paper tonight, or maybe what you'll read tomorrow night. The police pick up a lot of clues of various kinds, and it takes a while for them to get them sorted out. Sometimes things break fast, and sometimes they never break. They might be ready for an arrest tonight, or they might not know where to start."

From the kitchen came the cheerful sound of coffee percolating. She glanced at her watch. "It would be a terrible thing, wouldn't it, if someone did something like that and got away with it."

"They won't get away with it. Carter City has a good police force."

She set up a folding table, and brought the coffee in, and a plate of cookies. She sat at the other end of the sofa and munched cookies, and he sipped his coffee black and listened politely while she talked about Betty and Marilyn.

"They were nice kids," she said. She'd had lots of fun with them. "Why only last Monday...."

"You had dinner at the Carter Restaurant," Webber said. "And then you went to a movie."

She looked startled. "How did you know?"

"Several people have told me about that. Marilyn Andrews, for one."

"Marilyn? But—oh. You mean in the restaurant this noon. After I left."

He nodded.

"You investigators frighten me. Isn't there anything you don't find out?"

"Too many things." Such as, he thought, the reason you asked me over here tonight.

"I hope you haven't been prying into my past." She smiled as if the suggestion that she had a past was very funny.

"No reason to. At least, there hasn't been any reason so far. All I'm concerned with is that insurance application. I'd like to know something about the person that used Betty Parnet's name, but I know that wasn't you."

"What could a person gain by doing something like that?"

"I don't know. When the police figure that out, they'll probably find her—find her murderers."

"Terrible," she murmured. She reached for another cookie. "There. That's the last one, and I don't think you had one. When I get upset about something, I eat too much."

He asked her who had worked in the office on Saturday, and she didn't know but thought she could find out easily enough. "Is it important?" she said.

"Not particularly. It's just another detail. We have to check all the details."

"I'll ask."

Webber set down his coffee cup, and leaned back. The coffee wasn't helping, and he was afraid of suddenly dropping off to sleep. He wondered how she would react to a sleeping man on her sofa, and decided that he didn't care. To get out of the place gracefully—that was the problem.

"I know Betty didn't have any family," she said. "But Marilyn did, and her mother must be terribly worried. I know just how she feels. My mother died when I was twelve, and I practically brought up my brother and sister. I thought my life was finished when my brother was killed in World War II, and if anything happened to my sister—well, I know how Marilyn's mother must be feeling."

"Didn't Marilyn say something about her mother being sick?"

"That makes it even worse."

"All we can do is hope for the best," Webber said. "And—I'm afraid—expect the worst."

She shuddered, and sat up stiffly. He saw her hands were trembling, and she clasped them together and said, "The poor kid. It's terrible."

She lurched to her feet, and Webber was totally unprepared for what happened next. She dropped onto the sofa beside him, threw her arms around him, and pulled him toward her. As he tried to pull back, she pressed her lips fiercely against his and held him. Her strength, and the violence of the embrace, shocked him. Her eyes were closed, her face flushed. He wondered if one glass of weak wine could have done it.

He jerked his head away, and she pressed her cheek against his chest, and murmured, "Darn the lights. Want to do me a favor?"

"What—what's that?"

"Unbutton my dress."

Webber gripped her wrists firmly, and released himself. He stood up, and she stared at him, wide-eyed. There was something about her expression, something about her eyes, that defied interpretation. He was tempted to label it nymphomania, but he had a hunch that nothing about Ruth Johnson could be explained so simply.

"Sorry," he said. "I got practically no sleep last night, and I've had a frightfully eventful day. It's time I got to bed."

She looked suggestive in the direction of her bedroom, and held out her arms. "Murders, troubles—let's just forget them. For a little while."

Her voice quavered. Her eyes were staring wildly. In a flash of intuition he understood. The woman was frightened. More than frightened—she was terrified.

He shook his head. "Thank you for the information. And your hospitality. I'll probably see you at the office tomorrow."

She followed him to the door. "Do you really have to go?"

She was only an inch taller than he, but she seemed to tower over him.

He backed through the doorway cautiously. "I really must. Good night."

"Good night," she said, and closed the door softly.

Webber made his descent a frantic dash for the safety of the fresh night air. He walked toward his car, and a figure stepped out of the shadows. Webber chuckled, and punched him playfully.

"You really draw the assignments, eh McGowan?"

"You said it." He jerked his head towards the house. "Everything all right?"

'You might call it that."

"Bob wants you to give him a call. He'll be at home."

"All right. When I get home. Do you have an all-night job here?"

"We might. Think there's any chance of someone pulling the girl out of bed?"

"Not if it's a male," Webber said. "She'll pull him in with her."

He climbed into his car, and McGowan walked around and leaned on the door. "I don't suppose you dug up a few good leads tonight, or maybe solved this mess for us."

"Nope. Too bad you don't know the girl better. She just made some fresh coffee."

McGowan swore, and Webber waved, and drove away.

He drove warily, but he soon reassured himself. He was not being followed. Mrs. Mahoney had left the porch light on, and he parked in his usual parking place in front of the house, and started up the walk.

A voice hissed at him out of the darkness. "Webber?"

Webber dove to the ground, rolled, and came up behind a bush, cursing the light. He expected bullets, but there were none. There was only the nervous tranquility of a city residential street—the bus at the corner, a train whistling off somewhere, and small, reassuring domestic noises. He recognized the boom of Mrs. Mahoney's television, and from the open basement window of the house next door came the pat, pat, pat of a ping pong game.

The voice said again, "Webber? Now where the hell—"

A familiar voice answered, from directly behind Webber.

"He's over here, displaying an unfortunately impetuous scrupulosity. Do you mistrust our motives, Master Webber?"

Webber got to his feet resignedly, and brushed himself off. The familiar voice materialized into a specter of a man, a grotesquely tall and thin Prof Pronk, who bent over him helpfully.

"He's just a little squirt," the other said. "Do we call him Junior?"

Webber finished the brushing off, and drew himself up to his full five feet five. "You do at your own risk."

Pronk threw up his arms in mock alarm. "Are you both suspicious and voracious in one evening, Master Webber? Do you threaten us with bodily harm?"

"I may not be very tall," Webber said, "but I wouldn't have any trouble reaching your shins."

"I wouldn't dream of denying it."

They stood on the walk in front of the house, Pronk and his cohort keeping their backs to the light and their faces shadowed.

"Company approaches," Pronk said. "We had wistfully hoped to converse with you without interference from your guardian angels, but that is now impossible. We bring you an invitation from a kind, elderly gentleman who desires to make your acquaintance. Will you favor us with company?"

Two men had gotten out of the parked car and hurried toward them. They slowed their pace as they approached.

"Does your kind, elderly man have a name?" Webber asked.

"He does. But his closest friends call him something else."

The newcomers reached the light, and Webber recognized a detective.

"Isn't it time you were in bed, Simmons?" he asked.

"These guys giving you trouble?" Simmons growled.

"I can't honestly say that they are," Webber said.

"A veracious man!" Pronk murmured. "See how he stands out among us?"

"Downtown, we got a special cell for wise guys," the detective said.

Pronk smiled, and bowed from the waist. "So exceedingly regretful that I do not qualify."

Webber turned his back on the detective. "I think, gentlemen, we would have fewer interruptions inside."

"Better be careful, Webber," the detective said. "These guys—"

"I know," Webber said. "They don't go to church regularly. Do you?"

He strode toward the house, and Pronk, treading on his heels, remarked softly, "That was gross defamation of character."

Webber led them up the stairway, unlocked the door of his apartment, and flipped on the lights. He waved in the direction of the sofa. "Make yourselves comfortable."

Pronk immediately stretched out full length, with his long legs protruding over the end of the sofa. He was wearing the same black suit, white shirt, and black bow tie he'd had on the previous evening. He kicked off his shoes, revealing brilliant red and green striped socks under his black trousers. His companion found a chair for himself, and watched him disgustedly.

Webber brought three bottles of beer, passed them around, and seated himself across the room. "Gentlemen," he said, "And I use the title only out of politeness, did you come to apologize for your bad marksmanship of this afternoon?"

Pronk swung to a sitting position, and took a long drink of the beer. His sharply-protruding Adam's apple jerked comically. He lowered the bottle, smacking his lips. "Your dastardly assailants were not of us," he said.

"Do you perchance drive a blue sedan?"

"Perchance no."

"A brown sedan?"

Pronk's mouth drooped mournfully. "That was unkind of

you—most unkind. It is assuredly not playing the game to ring in a traffic policeman on your side."

"Then it was you that I took on that sightseeing trip to the Carter City Manufacturing Company?"

"I must humbly confess. We, and your guardian angels, were caught flatfooted by your friend the flatfoot."

Webber rubbed his forehead. "I'm not my brilliant self, this evening. What's this about guardian angels?"

"Do you mean, Master Webber, that you did not know you had guardian angels?"

"I did not."

"It distresses me to hear it. Spiritual things must be beyond you. Allow me to capitulate. We first sighted your studious countenance this morning over on Sunset Boulevard. A formal greeting was not practicable under the circumstances, for which I offer all due apologies."

"What were you doing on Sunset Boulevard?"

"An admirable question for the proper time and place, of which this is neither. When you left Sunset Boulevard, the previously mentioned blue sedan started off in pursuit. Its occupants were not among our unfortunately limited circle of acquaintances. Your guardian angels, who draw their pay from the fair city of Carter City when they are not otherwise occupied, set off in pursuit of the blue sedan. The situation seemed so intriguing that we followed the guardian angels."

"Damn!" Webber said. "You mean the police have been following me all day?"

"Not all day, though they have sniffed at your heels rather persistently. It was marvelous sport while it lasted, but on two occasions you proved too much for us."

"I had *three* tails?"

"Unnatural sounding, but true. From Sunset Boulevard to Charles Street you had three tails, if you insist on putting it thus vulgarly, except for the brief interval when you made your tour of Green Circle. Then you lost the blue sedan, and your guardian angels seemed momentarily more interested in the sedan than in you. Then you foolishly stopped to make a telephone call, and recaptured your caravan intact."

"After you left Charles Street, you lost the blue sedan, and since your guardian angels were sniffing the exhaust trail of the sedan, and we were following your guardian angels at a discrete distance, it inevitably resulted in your abandoning all three of us. We were not aware of this development until your guardian angels also lost the blue sedan, admitted defeat, and led us to police headquarters. Since we have no friends there, we followed them no longer."

"Then you weren't around when I was shot at," Webber said.

"Unfortunately, no. It must have been a wonderfully entertaining spectacle. We next joined your entourage later in the afternoon, when you left the National Bank Building with your friend, the detective. At that time you had regained your guardian angels, but not the blue sedan. We had small confidence in the efficacy of angels, after their sorry performance of the morning, so we slipped in ahead of them. But all went for naught when you played that foul prank with the police assistance. Are you sufficiently enlightened?"

"No," Webber said, "but thanks anyway."

"I shall now repeat the invitation which I was tendering when we were so rudely interrupted. A kind, elderly gentleman would like to make your acquaintance. Will you favor us with your company?"

"Your kind, elderly gentleman still has no name?"

"Most assuredly he has a name, but it is his own property. I never deal in other people's names."

"Now that I think about it, you've never dealt in your own name, either."

"For an entirely different reason," Pronk said. "I'm modest."

"I don't suppose that your kind, elderly gentleman confides his business to you."

"To a mere bearer of invitations?"

"Do you blindfold me now, or after we get outside?"

"Master Webber! You do us a grave injustice."

Webber got to his feet. "All right, gentlemen—still using the term out of politeness—let's go."

Pronk beamed at him. "Splendid!"

"And since you're too modest to tell me your names, I'll have to make you a present of some. For obvious reasons, quite apart from the fact that I first met you in the Crow Bar, you are hereby dubbed Scarecrow."

"An infamous libel both on my person and on *Corvus brachyrhynchos*, which is a magnificent bird, and not easily frightened."

Webber turned to his companion, a squat, powerfully built man clothed in a brown suit that was both shabby and in need of pressing. Webber hoped that his face had seen better days. "You," he pronounced solemnly, "are Butch."

Butch grunted.

"Your exceedingly kind cooperation is as appreciated as it is unexpected," Pronk said.

"Don't mention it," Webber said. "I've always wanted to make the acquaintance of Mr. Nick Falcone."

A smile puckered Pronk's face, and for a fleeting instance his eyes lost their sadness. He solemnly raised his finger to his lips.

CHAPTER EIGHT

Pronk halted them at the foot of the stairs, and said to Webber, "I suggest that you duplicate your sly exit of earlier this evening."

"Why?"

"Your guardian angels will indubitably protest."

"Then you were around earlier this evening."

"We were. We parked on the next street and came through the back way. We observed your elusive ways with soul-shattering amusement."

"But you didn't follow me."

Pronk shook his head. "We were confident that you would return."

"You've been more or less following me all day, but you waited until just now to deliver your invitation. What's the matter? Shy?"

"We were merely waiting until you were unoccupied. Do we depart surreptitiously?"

"We do not," Webber said. "We go out the front door, and we go in my car. Any objections?"

"Manifestly not. But you must allow me to buy the gasoline."

The detective moved out of the shadows and intercepted them as they came down the walk. "Do you know these guys?" Webber asked.

"Darned right I know them."

"I'm going to call on a kind, elderly gentleman. Do you know who that is?"

"I do, and that isn't what I'd call him."

"You aren't going to warn me to stay home?"

"You go right ahead, and we'll follow you. There's a want out on him."

The silence was broken by Pronk thoughtfully clucking his tongue. "This alters the situation," he said. "The trip would be futile. He would no longer be where I expected to find him."

"You disappoint me," Webber said. "I was so looking forward to meeting him. But maybe I'll get some sleep tonight. Come on up, and I'll give you a note to this kind, elderly gentleman, thanking him for the invitation."

The detective growled, "Me and my big mouth."

"I gravely fear," Pronk said, "That you will never make sergeant. But do not take it ruefully. Following us would have been discouragingly unproductive."

They returned to the house, with the detective looking after them suspiciously. Webber spun a piece of paper into the typewriter, and wrote, "Dear kind, elderly gentleman: Thank you so much for the invitation. Some other time, perhaps." He signed his name and handed it to Pronk.

"That's in case my guardian angels search you on the way out."

"I shall voluntarily allow them to read it," Pronk promised. "They seem desperately in need of edification."

"In about an hour, I'll sneak out the back way, and meet you on the next street. Wear a white carnation."

"I shall. I shall wear two of them, in my hair."

From the window, Webber watched Pronk flourish the paper under the nose of the detective. He pulled down his shades, turned on the radio and reached for a magazine.

Five minutes later he threw it aside, and seated himself at his desk. He took out a piece of paper, and ruled it into three columns. The columns he headed with the names of Betty Parnet, Marilyn Andrews, and Mrs. Lamont. At the top, he wrote "Suspects."

"All we have to do," he told himself, "is to find a name

common to all three columns, and then...."

Leaning back, he submerged himself in thought. Ten minutes later he crossed out "Suspects," and wrote, "Motive." Under Marilyn Andrews and Mrs. Lamont, he wrote, "Silence." Under Betty Parnet, he wrote, "Money—Howard."

And a long series of question marks.

"Too simple," he said. "And too obvious. But if Howard doesn't figure in it, who does? And why?

The murder of Betty Parnet was the key to the puzzle. Solve it, and the others would fall into place naturally. Frank Milford's murder, too, because the motive there was also silence.

He crumpled the paper, aimed at the wastebasket, and missed. From across the room Frank Milford's angel leered at him. "You know something?" Webber said. "You look a little like Scarecrow."

At the end of an hour, he went down and knocked on Mrs. Mahoney's door. She peeked out cautiously, and invited him in. She wore an all-enveloping white nightgown, which gave her a ghost-like appearance in the dim hallway.

"I knew you got back all right," she said. "I heard you come in."

"I got back all right, and now I need to ask you another favor."

"Mercy! They still after you?"

"It's the police, this time," Webber said. "But don't worry. I'm innocent."

She obediently put out all the lights at the rear of the house, and Webber slipped out of the darkened house into a darker night. He made it to the next street without incident, whistled softly, and was guided over to a parked car by an answering whistle.

Scarecrow had the motor running by the time Webber had climbed into the back seat. They drove off without lights.

"I don't see the carnations," Webber said.

"They're law-abiding carnations," Scarecrow said. "They close up after dark."

At the first intersection, Scarecrow flipped on his lights, and turned. He followed a meandering path as he checked and rechecked to see if he was being followed. Satisfied, he turned south on Miller Street, which soon became Ridge Road and took them around Suicide Curve and out into the country.

"I take it that you've relocated this kind, elderly gentleman," Webber said.

Neither of them answered.

"I hope you telephoned for instructions. I'm missing some sleep I need, and I won't think kindly of you if this gentleman isn't where he's supposed to be."

"When there's a want out on Big Nick, nobody telephones," Butch said.

They rode for a time in silence. Scarecrow was suspicious of a car that appeared behind them, and he slowed until it pulled out and passed. He said over his shoulder, "What slanderous accusations are the police making?"

"They haven't confided in me. Suspicion of murder, probably, suspicion of kidnapping, maybe, with no limit on the assorted lesser charges."

"They are resourceful in making their charges."

"But where Big Nick is concerned, not in proving them," Webber said.

"From your noble cooperation, I conclude that you do not share their suspicions."

"I don't know. I'm trying to put a puzzle together, and right now I'm looking for pieces. I'll have to handle Big Nick a little before I can say that he fits anywhere."

Scarecrow chuckled. "Please handle him with dignity. He is plummeting into the depths. The Parnet girl's death wounded him cruelly."

"I wondered about that," Webber said.

"Cruelly. To him she was a thing of beauty, the joy forever even when viewed from afar, the true passion that arrived, alas, but too late. At his tenderly advanced age that is a serious affliction. And by the way—Big Nick is not what the ink slingers would have you believe. He is genuinely a kind, elderly gentleman."

Scarecrow lapsed into silence. Webber made an unsuccessful attempt to engage Butch in conversation. Finally he leaned back, relaxed, and dozed off. When he jerked back to wakefulness, they were leaving the highway. He recognized the winding dirt road as one of several which served summer cottages and permanent homes on Round Lake, which was Carter City's leading summer resort.

Webber expressed surprise. "If he wanted to hide, why didn't he take Echo Lake?"

"Nothing over there but fish," Butch said. "Big Nick hates fish. He likes to swim, and sun himself on the beach, and if there are some pretty girls in bathing suits he don't kick none."

The sky was overcast, but rain no longer threatened. They began to catch glimpses of the lake, calm and unruffled, when the moonlight would momentarily find a break in the clouds. Trees arched a tunnel over the road. They met no cars, and there were none following them.

The car skidded slightly in the sand as Scarecrow turned off the road. A small frame cottage showed in the headlights, austere-looking, almost shabby. There was one other car in the driveway. The light in the cottage went off as Scarecrow brought the car to a stop. He raced his motor thunderously, and repeated the operation twice. The light came on again.

Scarecrow said cheerfully, "Follow the leader," and the two of them led him into the presence of Big Nick Falcone.

There were two other men in the room, but Webber saw only their backs as they disappeared through the opposite doorway. Scarecrow leaned against the wall, and folded his arms. Butch turned his back and rested his elbows on a window sill, looking absently at his reflection in the glass.

Stale smoke and whiskey fumes blended in the small room. There were a few much-abused pieces of furniture. The linoleum on the floor was worn and cracked. Webber paused in the middle of the room, and faced the man in the far corner.

He wore a stylish, black-satin dressing gown which carelessly revealed very unstylish underwear. He wore no shoes, and one of his socks needed darning. He was long overdue for a shave. Blood-shot eyes peered out of a pasty-white face, and his thick, silvery hair was drooping and tangled. He seemed shrunken and insignificant, huddled there in a worn overstuffed chair. Webber recalled a newspaper photo of a couple of weeks before, Big Nick Falcone triumphantly leaving the courtroom, hands clasped over his head for the benefit of the photographers, and shook his head.

Big Nick rested a glass on the coffee table at his right knee, and squinted at Webber. There were bottles on the table, some of them full and some of them with varying degrees of emptiness. Big Nick refilled his glass, and drained it convulsively.

His voice was blurred and wheezy. "What was Betty Parnet to you?"

"A name," Webber said.

"Sit down."

Webber did not move.

Falcone shouted hoarsely. "Sit down!"

"Ask me politely," Webber said, "and I'll consider it."

Falcone's fingers tightened on his glass. Before he could speak, Scarecrow's sonorous voice interrupted. "Mr. Webber," he said softly, "is a gentleman, and he plays square." He described their elusion of the police, and Falcone kept his eyes on Webber, and nodded from time to time.

When Scarecrow had finished, Falcone said almost gently, "Have a chair. Please."

"Thank you," Webber said, and sat down. He had ideas of his own as to how the interview should proceed from that point. "I suppose you read in the paper that Betty Parnet was murdered. Did the paper say why?"

Falcone shook his head.

Choosing his words carefully, Webber told him about the insurance policy. Falcone refilled his glass, and then sat motionless, holding it in front of him. He was silent for a long time.

"Why do the police think I killed her?" he said finally.

"When a girl gets murdered, any male connected with her gets a careful look. In this case, you're the only one eligible."

"I loved that girl, Webber. I'd have gladly committed murder for her, but I wouldn't have harmed her. Oh, she was never interested in me—that way. Said I was like a father to her and called me 'Dad.' She never knew her own father. And when she found out what I really am, she wouldn't have anything to do with me. I never blamed her."

"What about Mrs. Lamont?" Webber said. "Did you love her too?"

Falcone's face went blank. "Who the hell is that?"

"Former landlady of Betty Parnet. Charles Street."

"Oh." Falcone's shoulders drooped wearily. "What does that old battle ax have to do with it?"

"The police kind of think you murdered her too."

"She was murdered?" Falcone said. He turned to Scarecrow. "Was that in the paper?"

Scarecrow nodded.

"No reason for me to hurt her. Sure, we had a run-in once. I got Betty to drink some champagne. She'd never had anything stronger than ginger ale, and it made her sick. When I took her home, that old battle ax climbed all over me. And that was the last time Betty ever went out with me. The old girl put the idea into her head that I got her sick on purpose. My God! I just wanted to make her happy. Champagne wasn't good enough for her. But I think the old lady liked Betty, and was trying to look out for her. I shouldn't have got her drunk that night. But I didn't know...."

The glass wavered dangerously. Falcone set it down, sank lower in his chair, and buried his face in his hands. Webber lit a cigarette, and tossed one to Scarecrow. Butch continued to stare unseeing out of the window.

With Falcone on the defensive, Webber fired questions relentlessly. Falcone had met Betty Parnet at the Ronson and Wilcox offices. Wilcox was his lawyer, and had masterminded

Falcone's defense in his latest brush with the law. Falcone knew Ronson only slightly, thought he was a good lawyer, but did not care for him personally. Falcone had a nodding acquaintance with William J. Howard. He did not know that Howard was Betty Parnet's uncle.

"He was also the beneficiary on that life insurance policy I was telling you about," Webber said.

Falcone straightened up quickly. The glass smashed to the floor, and spread its contents over the linoleum. "Webber, if I thought Howard did that...."

"Don't. So far there's nothing that even hints that he did. He was another of Wilcox's clients, wasn't he?"

"Used to be."

"Isn't any longer?"

"They had a spat about something. Politics, I think. Wilcox is a big gun in politics, but he's an old-line party man and always has been. Howard was thinking about running for mayor as an independent reform candidate. I heard there was a big blow up."

"Is Howard still thinking about it?"

"I don't know. Politics isn't my line. What does this have to do with Betty?"

"You tell me. Did you know a girl named Marilyn Andrews?"

Falcone shook his head.

"Works for Ronson and Wilcox, and shared an apartment with Betty. She knew something about Betty's murder. As a result, she disappeared."

Falcone was obviously uninterested. "I'd like to make a deal with you, Webber."

"Do you want to find Betty Parnet's murderer?"

"You can make a cool grand without any trouble. If you find out who did that to Betty, just give me a couple of hours head start on the police. I'll save the city some money."

"Do you want to find Betty Parnet's murderer?"

Falcone stared at him dully.

"Marilyn Andrews knows who it was. That's why she was kidnapped."

"The devil! What'd she look like?"

Webber described her. "I might be able to get ahold of a photo for you," Webber said.

"Do that," Falcone said. "I'll put the boys on it."

"Any out-of-town crooks been in Carter City lately?"

Falcone bristled. "This is my territory, Webber. I don't allow outsiders."

"You didn't answer the question."

"The answer is no!"

Webber stood up. "I thank you for the interview, Mr. Falcone. I think it's been instructive for both of us." He walked across the room, and gripped Falcone's limp hand. "I'll get that photo for you."

As he went out the door, he had a last glimpse of Falcone filling another glass. Scarecrow was wrong, Webber thought. Falcone was not a kind, elderly gentleman. He was an untidy, broken old man.

Or perhaps he was a consummate actor. Webber found this idea intriguing.

Scarecrow was the sole escort on the return trip, and drove without talking until they got off the dirt road and onto the highway. He made his turn, glanced sideways, and said, "Tough. Really and truly unfortunate. If she had married some nice young man and raised a family and lived happily ever after, Big Nick could have taken it without flinching. He'd even have been godfather to the kids, and considered it an honor. This way, it's almost too much for him."

"Are you an actor, too?" Webber said.

"You speak in perplexities."

"No. I only think in perplexities. Did anyone ever tell you that you almost talk normally, on occasion?"

"No one has ever been so rude as to suggest that I ever talk abnormally."

He sounded hurt. Almost, Webber thought, like a small child who has had his fingers slapped. Webber smiled. "It's rather a good act. How did you happen to pick it up?"

They were approaching Suicide Curve, and Scarecrow slowed carefully. "I've never had a ride on a roller coaster. I just thought of that. I'll have to do that some time."

"I'll go along and hold your hand. But not tonight."

Scarecrow went on, talking softly. "I think I was about six years old. My mother supported us by doing laundry, and one of her customers was a college professor. She took me along one day. He had a room full of books. I'd never had a book of my own. But—" His voice snapped back to normal, resonant and ironic. "—I have all the books I want, now. I have more books than that professor. I have time to read them, too."

"Hail, *Britannica*," Webber said.

"I have the *Americana*, too."

"How does a character like you fit in with Falcone and company?"

"Are you contemplating my reformation, Master Webber? Pray don't. Carter City wears an aura of calm. Do you suppose there have been any murders during our absence?"

"This is one of the many times I've been glad my dad didn't make a policeman out of me," Webber said. "It's nice to have nothing more than an insurance application to worry about."

Whereupon he folded his arms, watched Miller Avenue rolling by, and commenced to worry about murder. And a kidnapping.

"Do you elect an undignified approach from the rear?" Scarecrow said.

"I think I do. Thanks. If I go in the front, the guardian angels may want to know where and how."

"I believe it would be wise."

Scarecrow cut his lights as soon as he'd edged into a parking place, and as Webber reached for the door, he felt Scarecrow's hand on his arm.

"Just a moment," Scarecrow said. "Would you extinguish your cigarette, please? Thank you. We must talk, you and I."

"Any particular subject?"

"Several. I like you Master Webber. You are indeed an

expert. Never have I heard Big Nick answer so many questions in so short a time. By temperament, Big Nick prefers to ask questions. Your technique is admirable."

"That's my job," Webber said. "Asking questions."

"You are also modest. And honest. Which makes it doubly unfortunate that Big Nick chose to tell you an outrageous falsehood."

Because there seemed to be nothing for him to say, Webber made no comment.

"This conversation is to remain a small confidence between us. Do what you like with what I say, but forget where you heard it."

"A little bird told me," Webber said.

"*Corvus brachyrhynchos*," Scarecrow murmured. "Excellent."

"Are you going to tell me that Falcone murdered Betty Parnet and Mrs. Lamont, and kidnapped Marilyn Andrews?"

"To the best of my knowledge, Big Nick had no part in any of those foul crimes."

"But he did lie to me?"

"He spoke with questionable veracity when he answered your well-placed question concerning a non-resident criminal element in Carter City. There are to my certain knowledge a half-dozen such unsavory characters contaminating our fair city at this moment. If Big Nick were his usual forceful self he would have handled the matter. Unfortunately, he discovered this fact shortly after he heard of the untimely demise of his beloved, and he has been unable to cope with any problem more complex than opening a bottle. The said characters have assured him that they are here on a private matter, and will leave promptly when it is properly consummated."

"Why do you tell me this?"

"Because I like you, Master Webber. And because you have already met two of these characters. They were driving a blue sedan today. Tomorrow they will be driving something else. It is not proper that such maladjusted personalities should roam our streets making attempts on the lives of respectable citizens."

Webber smiled, and if Scarecrow did not see the expression, he sensed it. "I will remind you, Master Webber, that Big Nick does not use violence. He has surrounded himself with men of considerable callosity, but that is to create the proper illusion. This crass invasion must be dealt with, and I am assuming that you will pass the information along where it will be most useful."

"I don't suppose you can furnish names, or descriptions."

"I know only one of the brigands by name. It's a last name, and I'm certain it is only one of the many names he chooses to employ. It is Morton."

"Morton," Webber mused. "Morton. Now that is odd."

"I have certain knowledge that he has made himself extremely unwelcome in Chicago, so much so that the Chicago police would very much like to have him back."

"Morton," Webber said again. "You sure it wasn't Martin?"

"He may call himself Martin from time to time, but I have never heard him called anything but Morton."

"I see. Are you equally positive that you haven't been talking with an attractive young lady named Marilyn Andrews?"

"I beg your pardon?"

"Let it pass," Webber said.

"As for Miss Andrews—if you will obtain a photo for me, I shall see what I can do."

"Thanks. How'll I get it to you?"

"Leave it with that cooperative landlady of yours. For a scarecrow."

"All right. If I can get one, I'll leave it with her."

Webber opened the door, and said lightly, "Until the next time...."

Scarecrow replied, "Caw."

Webber made his way home through the back yard, tapped softly at Mrs. Mahoney's window, and received a joyful welcome. The lights were still on in his room. The radio was still playing loudly. He raised the shade, and looked down onto the street, wondering if his guardian angels were stuck for the night. It seemed ridiculous, and the more he thought about it, the madder it made him.

The telephone rang. He took his time answering it, and Hendricks drawled, "Did I wake you up?"

"When I'm fully awake, I'll tell you."

"That's what I figured. I've been waiting for you to call. Have any luck with the girl?"

"I'll discuss the matter with you after you call off the dogs who are snoozing on my door step. No sooner."

Hendricks was silent for a moment. "I didn't put them there," he said. "But I'll see what I can do. I'll call you back."

It took him ten minutes. "They're called off," he announced. "Look—I hear Nick Falcone wanted to see you."

"So I was told."

"You did the smart thing."

"Generous of you to admit it."

"Get anything from the Johnson girl?"

"She doesn't think the man's name was Martin."

"Neither do I. Martin has alibis. We're still checking, though. Does she suggest a substitute?"

"Why don't you ask Nick Falcone for a suggestion?"

"I will, as soon as they bring him in. Which should be in about twenty minutes."

"Ah!"

"We had an anonymous tip half an hour ago. A phone call. He's hiding out in a cottage on Round Lake. The state police are moving in now."

"I see. Here's another anonymous tip for you. Ask the Chicago police if they know anything about a man named Morton."

Hendricks sputtered. "Where...?"

"Anonymous. Don't bother me before noon tomorrow."

Webber hung up. He sat at Frank Milford's desk, and thumbed his nose at the angel. "So Scarecrow told the truth," he said. "So there are some non-resident brigands in town."

CHAPTER NINE

The telephone jerked Webber out of a sound, dreamless sleep. He stumbled across the room and yawned a response. Scarecrow's voice lashed at him scornfully.

"Master Webber, you are a viper."

"Wrong," Webber said. "You wouldn't know a viper if you saw one. You've only gotten as far as M, and viper is a V."

"You are a viper. Nothing less would impose upon a host's courtesy and hospitality by slimily coiling its way to the police as soon as...."

"Whoa! You've got the wrong viper."

"You profess innocence?"

"If that means I didn't do it."

"I see. I rather thought not. The timing was off, for one thing. But Big Nick thought yes. Unfortunately, his thinking was conditioned by a night in abominable accommodations supplied by the police."

"Is he at liberty now?"

"At liberty and drowning his sorrows."

"Kindly inform Big Nick," Webber said, "That at the very moment of our memorable conversation the police were being informed of his whereabouts anonymously by telephone. And if Big Nick would like my personal opinion, these non-resident brigands...."

"Their hour of decision is at hand. Many thanks, Master Webber."

"About the photo of Marilyn Andrews...," Webber began,

and stopped because Scarecrow had hung up.

He called police headquarters. The police had a photo of Marilyn Andrews, and were happy to supply copies. Webber told them to deliver the copies to Mrs. Mahoney, and then he went downstairs and arranged to have Mrs. Mahoney pass them along to a man calling himself Scarecrow. He telephoned National Credit, and told Boyd he'd be no later than noon. He treated himself to a luxury of a leisurely breakfast. It was nine o'clock when he left the house, and the clock in the lobby of the National Bank building said nine-thirty as he was getting into the elevator.

Inside the door of the Ronson and Wilcox offices, he paused and looked for Ruth Johnson. The dark-haired girl Wilcox had called Sally was at the switchboard. She was handling an incoming call, and she seemed flustered. Webber stepped forward when she was free, and she smiled shyly at him.

"Where's Ruth this morning?" he asked

She sighed. "Late. I've never done this before, and it's confusing. I just got Providence Hospital for Mr. Wilcox when he wanted the Municipal Court Building, and he nearly ruptured my ear drums."

"He would," Webber said. "Would it confuse you more if I asked you a couple of questions?"

"I don't think so."

"Did you work last Saturday?"

She nodded, and Webber explained the problem. He wanted to find someone who could tell him the precise times Betty Parnet was in the office. Sally could, and did. She had been in the office with Betty all morning, they had gone to lunch together to a little coffee shop over on Lake Street, and they had been in the office together all afternoon.

"Splendid," Webber said. "Now—what about Monday morning? Was Betty in the office all morning?"

She nodded.

"And you were part of the Monday evening theatre party?"

She nodded again.

"I'll need your name and address," he said. He entered it into his notebook. Sally Landis. A Sunset Boulevard address, but three blocks down the street from where Betty Parnet had lived. "Would that all my tasks were so simple. Next I must tackle your bosses. Who is in the most receptive mood?"

"Mr. Ronson, usually," she said. "He's always polite. Mr. Wilcox is nice, but sometimes he loses his temper."

"Would you ask Mr. Ronson if he can spare a few minutes from his crowded schedule for an insurance investigator?"

She fussed at the board, spoke briefly, and turned with a smile. "You can go right in. That way. Yes—that's his office."

"Come in," Ronson called. He pushed some papers aside, and reached across the desk to take Webber's hand. "Sit down, please. You're still at it I see."

"But almost finished, I hope," Webber said, seating himself.

Ronson tilted back in his chair, and stroked a cheek thoughtfully with one finger. "The police aren't saying much, but I know this is a nasty business," he said. "And this thing about Marilyn—I owe the poor kid an apology. I thought she just ducked out to do some shopping. But—" He turned his palms up. "—what can I do for you?"

His light summer suit was immaculate. The hands he rested on his desk were as carefully cared for as those of a concert pianist. Webber's startled nostrils caught the faint scent of perfume. Ronson's, or had one of the office girls just left the room?

His eyes were alert and intelligent, his face almost ridiculously ugly. For cataloging Webber placed him mentally beside Falcone, Scarecrow and Howard, and decided that the lineup was getting absurd.

"I'm still on the Betty Parnet insurance application," he said. "It seems like ancient history, so much has been happening."

"Insurance application?" Ronson said. "I hadn't heard about that. The papers didn't mention it."

He lit a cigarette, and listened attentively as Webber explained.

"I see," he said. He frowned. "All you really want is proof that the application was fraudulent. No—you want overwhelming proof. I begin to see why someone took a shot at you yesterday. The papers weren't very explicit about that, either."

"I didn't see them," Webber said. He hoped he wouldn't have to start dodging reporters, now, on top of everything else. Evidently the police had toned down the report, or the press would have been camping on his doorstep. "We've established pretty well that the application was fraudulent. I'm only picking up a few loose ends to wind things up. What kind of character reference could Betty Parnet have gotten from your firm?"

"As far as I know, first rate. Understand—Wilcox hired her, and she worked on his business more than on mine. Each of us has a couple of girls who specialize. It makes for better efficiency."

"Would you say that her salary was large enough to permit her to spend fifteen hundred dollars a year for life insurance?"

"We pay our girls well, but not that well. And Betty had only been with us for about six months. Make it seven. We give the girls automatic raises at regular intervals, but Betty was still on starting salary."

"Do you know anything about Betty's relationship with her uncle?"

"I knew Howard was her uncle. Wilcox mentioned that, once. But that's all I knew."

"I see," Webber said. "I thought as long as Howard was a client of your firm...."

Ronson grinned. "Jim's client. I'm just a nodding acquaintance. Jim and Howard have been close friends for years—a lot of years. They have a row every now and then, and swear they'll never speak again, but it always blows over. But you said Howard was the beneficiary on that insurance policy. The police want to know whether Howard would try to kill his niece to collect the insurance. They didn't ask in so many words, but I can see, now, what they were after. The insurance company will want to know the same thing. I'm no expert on human behavior, but I don't think Howard murdered his niece. I don't know him well enough to say he wouldn't commit murder, but I doubt that he'd do it for money. He can make thirty-five thousand dollars in so many easier and safer ways, if he needs it, and he doesn't need it. Why he was considering going into politics, a short time back, and there wasn't even any talk about a campaign fund. He just didn't need any contributions."

"Is he still considering going into politics?"

"As far as I know, he is. But you'd better ask Jim about that. Jim knows the details."

Webber got to his feet. "Thank you. It's generous of you to give me your time, especially with your office being short-handed. I imagine things are pretty confused."

"We'll make out. Glad to be of help. You'll want to talk to Jim, though, since Betty was his secretary. Here—I'll take you over."

Webber agreed gratefully. They started across the outer office, and Ronson stopped to talk to Sally. "Isn't Ruth here yet?" he asked.

Sally shook her head.

"Now I've heard everything," Ronson said. "After half past, isn't it? When was the last time Ruth was late?"

"I don't remember. I'm sure she would have called if she were sick. And no one answers at her apartment, so she must be on her way."

Ronson walked on, but Webber hesitated, and a chill feeling danced its way down his spinal column. He said firmly, "I think you'd better get police headquarters for me."

Sally looked startled, but she pointed to an empty desk, and told him, "You can use that phone."

She put the call through, and with the office force looking on and Ronson waiting with a puzzled look on his face, Webber asked for Hendricks. "Ruth Johnson," he said. "She hasn't shown at the office, and no one answers her phone."

"We're moving," Hendricks said, and cut off.

Ronson seemed amused. "Was that really necessary?"

Webber said seriously, "Yes, I think it was. You've had one

office girl murdered, and another one kidnapped. If everything is all right, it can't do any harm. If everything isn't all right, the less time lost, the better."

"Perhaps so. I don't specialize in criminal cases, you know, so I don't generally think in terms of violence until after the fact. Of course it doesn't do any harm."

As they reached Wilcox's office, his voice was rattling the door. "Sally, the telephone was invented in 1876. 1876, do you hear? And a thing that's been around that long ought to be understood by everyone. Just give me an open line, and I'll get him myself. In all the time I've been in business, you're the first person I've ever met who couldn't cope with a simple thing like a telephone. An open line...."

He slammed down the receiver as they walked in. "Jim," Ronson said, "Do this young man a favor. He has a job to finish up, and you're the last obstruction."

Wilcox leaned back, hooked his thumbs under his suspenders, and grinned. "What's on your mind, fellow?"

Ronson winked at Webber, and discretely slipped out the door. Webber took the chair beside Wilcox's desk, and came directly to the point. "What kind of character reference would you have given Betty Parnet?"

"The best one I could write," Wilcox said. "She was a fine gal to work with. Smart as a whip, capable. Tell her something once, and you could count on it being done. Her dictation was kind of shaky when she came here, but that was because she was inexperienced, and it didn't stay shaky long. She must have picked up her brains from Howard's side of the family."

As he said Howard's name, he scowled. Webber had been searching his mind desperately for the question he needed next, and he still hadn't found it. "As a friend of Mr. Howard's...," he began.

Wilcox's feet hit the floor. Red-faced, he pounded on his desk. "That double-crosser is no friend of mine!"

"Then you don't approve of his politics," Webber said politely.

"Listen here, fellow. A reflection on the party's honesty is a reflection on my honesty, and I won't stand for it. We've given Carter City a clean administration for years. I'm not saying that politicians don't turn out bad, sometimes, but the party has handled that sort of thing before, and it can handle it if it happens again. Reform mayor—phooey! Corruption in city contracts—phooey! This firm has acted as the city's attorney for the last seven years. If there was corruption, don't you think I'd know about it?"

Webber asked about Howard's relationship with his niece, worked in a question about Howard's financial status, and brought up the matter of the insurance application. Wilcox had not heard about it, and he did not seem interested until Webber mentioned that Howard was the beneficiary.

Then he grinned fiendishly. "You're too polite, fellow," he said. "What you really want to ask me is whether Bill Howard would get his niece knocked off to collect that thirty-five grand. Right?"

"I wouldn't phrase it precisely that way," Webber said.

"Nonsense. I know what you mean. You aren't asking me, 'Did he do it?' You're asking me, 'Is he the sort of person who would do it?' Even if he would, doesn't mean he did. Police have to prove those things. But don't quibble about language with a lawyer, fellow.

"Let's see. Would he do it? Good question. I'll give you a good answer. It wouldn't surprise me at all. Not at all."

Webber stopped in the outer office to talk with Sally. She was looking worried, now, and she told him she had called Ruth Johnson's apartment again, and a policeman had answered.

"Should I have called the police sooner?" she said. "I didn't think it was anything serious. I thought maybe she just over-slept. Las night was her date night, you know, and I haven't any idea what hours she kept when she had a date."

Webber reassured her. "There wasn't any reason for you to think something was wrong. A million different things could have made her late. And we still don't know that there's anything to worry about."

"Gee, I hope she's all right," she said. She turned suddenly, and from her nervous movements Webber guessed that Wilcox was trying to get another number.

It was five blocks to the Star Mutual Life office. It was three blocks in the opposite direction where Webber had left his car. He balanced off thirteen blocks of walking against a half-hour search for a parking place with the possibility of ending up at the same parking lot. He decided to walk.

For two blocks he made it a highly erratic walk, ducking in one door of a store and out another, wandering through a hotel lobby, turning a corner abruptly, and then waiting in sly ambush to see who would come charging after him. No one did, and he concluded that any tail he might have had gave up in disgust during the first block.

Henry Manning, the local manager for Star Mutual Life, wore a somewhat harassed expression. He led Webber through a bustling office, pausing once to settle a dispute between three agents who were contesting for the services of one stenographer. He closed the door of his private office with something closely resembling a sigh.

"We've been entertaining the police," he said. "It's put us at least a day behind schedule."

He was a big man, athletic-looking in spite of fifty years and his graying hair. The grin he gave Webber was not unfriendly. "I've been expecting you, though I must say I'm not unhappy that you waited until the police had gotten in their licks."

"I promise not to duplicate the police performance." Webber said. "Did you meet my friend Hendricks?"

"I never saw him before yesterday. Now he's an old acquaintance. It's just one of those things, I suppose. Jones is a good producer. He's only been with us two years, and he's going great. But he'll never make assistant manager."

"I don't see that the agent can be blamed in any way for what happened," Webber said. "There was nothing wrong with the application on the surface, and going below the surface is our responsibility, not his."

"I'm glad to hear you say that. I hope you'll say as much in your report."

"Certainly. Stopping this thing was our job. We stopped it. Star Mutual has no basis for complaint. The first thing I want is the timing on the application. I imagine the police have already gone into that."

"And how! Well—Jones wrote the application on Saturday. He didn't turn it in until Monday, because we closed at noon on Saturday. Frankly, I'm surprised that he didn't come charging back here waving it joyfully as soon as he wrote it, but he had a couple of important appointments."

"So he held onto all that cash over the weekend."

"I raked him over a little on that one. We have a general account at the First National, and they're open until five on Saturday. He should have deposited the money, and turned in a deposit slip. But he didn't, and he did turn in the money, so there was no harm done there."

"Did he deduct his commission?"

Manning said firmly, "None of my men deduct commissions. Some managers allow that, but not this one. The agent who deducts commissions will never have much of a payday, and every man should have a payday. All of my men remit gross. Where were we? Oh. Jones turned in the application Monday morning. It was recorded, and it went out to the company in the morning mail. The requisition for the inspection report went out in the morning mail. More than that I do not know."

'What line was Hendricks following?"

"Our employees, past and present. He wanted to know everyone who had worked for us in any capacity in the last five years. It was a big order. We have the usual trouble with office girls getting married or quitting for various reasons. And then there is the agent turnover. This is a big territory, and we have to have a growing field force. And we have to hire and train about three agents to find one good man who can make a real success of the business. Don't tell me you want to go into that."

"No. Hendricks is welcome to it. Did anyone around this office happen to know Betty Parnet?"

"There's another odd one. I told Hendricks no, never heard of her before. And then darned if she didn't turn up in our files. She applied for a job in March of last year. One of our girls was going to quit, and then she changed her mind so we didn't hire anyone. We kept Parnet's application on file so she could be called for any future openings, which is our usual procedure."

"Could I see her application?" Webber asked.

"Certainly. Just a moment."

He darted away, and returned with a mimeographed question-naire, neatly filled in. Webber examined it curiously, checking the data given there against the data given in the application for insurance. He found no discrepancy.

"You see the implications, don't you?" he said. "Whoever had access to this could have used the information in applying for insurance in Betty Parnet's name. Everything needed to complete a life insurance application is given here. Even her signature, if someone felt like forgery. I suppose Hendricks saw this?"

Manning grinned. "He photographed it."

"Then one line of his investigation will be the possibility of someone in this office being connected with the insurance fraud. Of course the same thing would be true of any place Betty Parnet has worked in Carter City, and possibly of any place she applied for work. I don't envy the police."

"Neither do I. I don't like sitting smack on top of one of those lines of investigation, but here I am."

"If you can let me use your phone for a few minutes, I won't bother you further."

Webber called police headquarters. Ruth Johnson had not been located. He called Mrs. Mahoney. The pictures had been delivered, and a man identifying himself as Scarecrow had called and picked them up.

"Did he leave any message for me?" Webber asked.

With a strange inflection in her voice, she replied, "He said to tell you—'Caw.'"

Webber hung up thoughtfully.

"How are things breaking?" Manning asked.

"I'd say that the police aren't doing so well. As fast as they get one finger in the dike, there's a spectacular washout somewhere else. But me—" He leaned back, and stretched luxuriously. "—I'm finished. All I have to do now is write it up."

He returned to the National Credit Company office, and it was precisely noon when he ripped the last sheets out of his typewriter, and separated the carbons. He uttered a loud, "Hurrah!"

Doris dropped a filing drawer. Boyd hurried to the door of his office, and stared.

Webber presented the report ceremoniously. "I'm ready to go back to work," he said.

Boyd turned, and picked up a stack of inspection requisitions from his desk. "I know you've done a good job. I'd give you the rest of the day off, if we weren't short-handed. But—you can start with these."

Webber returned to his desk, and went to work on the requisitions. Doris finished sorting the morning mail, and carried it in to Boyd. Silence reigned only briefly, to be shattered by a bellow from Boyd's office.

"Webber!"

Webber went in a rush. Boyd sat bolt upright, excitement lighting his face. He had left his glasses on. He held a pink requisition slip with one hand, and pointed with the other. He swallowed several times before he found his voice.

"Another thirty-five thousand dollar case," he croaked. "And look at the beneficiary."

Webber looked. The beneficiary was William J. Howard.

"Community Life," Boyd said. "So we don't have to start another whirl with Star Mutual. Would you like to take this one on, or should I...."

"Move your thumb," Webber said.

Boyd obliged, and uncovered the name of the applicant. It was Ruth Johnson.

CHAPTER TEN

Mrs. Mahoney had an oversized cake waiting for Webber that evening. Hendricks arrived before he got around to sampling it, so Webber poured the detective a cup of coffee and stood with knife poised over the cake while Hendricks eyed it hungrily.

"My favorite," Webber said. "Chocolate, with nothing but whipped cream for frosting. Large piece or small?"

"That's the problem. If I take a large piece, I'll be a hog to ask for seconds. If I take a small piece, I can ask for seconds, but two small pieces might not add up to one large piece. How about a medium-sized piece?"

"I'll make it a large," Webber said. "And you can carve the seconds yourself. What's on your mind?"

"They tell me you're not on this latest thing."

Webber shook his head, and talked with a mouthful of cake. "Boyd offered it to me. I respectfully declined. I want a flock of piddling little thousand-dollar cases until I catch up on my sleep. Frazier drew it, and he's a good man."

"This is the funniest case I've ever seen. We've had some good breaks, but every time we get our teeth into one, it turns out not to mean anything. For example—that tip of yours about a Morton was first rate. One of the prints we lifted from the car belonged to a man sometimes known as Morton, and Chicago wants him bad for assorted mayhem. They rushed us some photos, and we've already gotten a positive identification. Morton sold Betty Parnet the car. But where does that leave us?

Morton could be in Mexico by now, and I'm certain that the brains that set this mess in motion were local brains.

"Then there's this Ruth Johnson business. I called the boys in at seven this morning, and not too long after that the woman downstairs heard an argument in Johnson's apartment. It seemed pretty violent, but it didn't last long, so she didn't think any more about it until we came along. But Johnson's apartment is a mild mess, and she hasn't been seen or heard of since."

"Was the place searched?"

Hendricks shook his head. "Just a small rough-house. Like someone wanted her to go, and she wanted to stay. That argument may be a clue. It makes me think she knew the person, or persons. With a stranger she would have screamed for help, maybe, but not argued."

"Then we have an assortment of odds and ends. We have our first lead on Marilyn Andrews. A newsboy saw her getting into a car shortly after one o'clock. Right in front of the National Bank building. He identified Andrews from her picture, but the driver of the car was a woman, and he didn't know who she was."

"The second appearance of the mystery woman," Webber said.

"Second? You mean fourth. Fifth. The insurance agent, the two doctors, your friend Greenway, and now the newsboy. The woman's description matches, too. And speaking of Greenway, did you know he has suddenly become wealthy? He's been in a financial jam. He has a big family and a wife who doesn't seem to manage very well, and he's been owing a lot of people for a long time. Suddenly on Tuesday he went out and paid off a flock of those bills. He told us he'd saved up the money."

"I wouldn't have thought it," Webber said. "Did you say anything to Boyd?"

"In an oblique way. I think there was a payoff, but darned if I can see what he was paid off for. The only thing he really missed in his report was Mrs. Lamont's bit about Nick Falcone, and that wasn't entirely his fault. And it wasn't his fault if some dame passed herself off as a person he'd never seen before. He took all the usual precautions, Boyd says, and the job he did is above average. Got any ideas?"

Webber shook his head silently.

"Then there's this latest insurance application. I thought when Boyd called that I'd find something along the same pattern as the Parnet application, but I was wrong. For one thing, Johnson disappeared without seeing any doctors or investigators. And unlike the Parnet case, we're reasonably certain who it was who applied for the insurance."

"Another mysterious woman?"

"No. It was Ruth Johnson. Don't stare at me like that. Late yesterday afternoon she called the Community Life office and said she wanted some life insurance, and would they kindly send an agent around to her address about five thirty. The agent went, and wrote the application. He tore back to the office in wild glee, and got it processed the same evening. He's feeling sick, right now, but that's beside the point. The person he describes is Ruth Johnson, he has identified her from a photo, and we've established by way of neighbors that Ruth Johnson was home about that time. She must have called you from her apartment, right after the insurance agent left."

"How do you account for the presence of Howard as the beneficiary?"

Hendricks rubbed his hands together. "That's the most intriguing angle we've turned up yet. Howard and Ruth Johnson have been, for the past four years, performing an act in unison. You'd call it going steady. Stop staring. Howard's wife died six, seven years ago. They had no children. I don't know if Howard mourned the loss of feminine companionship. I rather doubt it. But he did mourn the loss of a capable bridge partner. He's one of those nuts about bridge, though he keeps his passion sternly under control and lets himself go only once a week. Four years ago he met Ruth Johnson in some way which he professes to have forgotten. She was a surprisingly capable bridge partner. He asked her out to play again, and it worked into a routine.

Every Wednesday evening, foul weather or fair, he takes her out to dinner at the New Carter Hotel, and afterwards they go to the Elks Club and play bridge in the guest room. Usually they play with the same elderly couple Howard has known and been playing bridge with for years."

"He would be a bridge fanatic," Webber said. "He'd be the kind of player who memorizes every card as it is played, and figures out the odds to the fourth decimal place."

"Could be. So, when friend Johnson decided to buy thirty-five thousand dollars' worth of life insurance, which she is no better able to afford than Parnet, naturally the first person she thought of as beneficiary was her old friend, William J. Howard. Anything wrong with that reasoning?"

"Everything. The insurance company wouldn't accept Howard as beneficiary. A beneficiary has to be a relative, or a person who would in some way suffer financial loss through the death of the insured person. Howard would have a tough time proving the loss of a bridge partner to be worth thirty-five thousand dollars. It was different with Parnet, since Howard was her only close relative."

"The Community Life man explained it to me more or less the same way. A small policy might get by with a friend named as beneficiary, but one as large as this one brings a quick inquiry as to the relationship with the friend. The agent put the question to Johnson, and she blushed, he says, and told him she and Howard were informally engaged. Whereupon as soon as the agent left, and as soon as she'd invited you over, she telephoned Howard and broke their dinner and bridge date for the first time in four years. It upset him completely, and he was still in a nasty mood this afternoon. He denies the part about being informally engaged, but he admits that if he decided to marry again, he'd probably do Johnson the honor. Good bridge partners are rare, you know. In the meantime, he's worried about missing next Wednesday's bridge date, too, and by heck we'd better find Johnson by then, or he's going to raise hell."

"Did Johnson pay cash down with the application?"

"One thousand, eight hundred and eighty dollars and ninety cents. It's the same kind of a policy, though. Retirement at age sixty."

"Johnson is older than Parnet was, which would make for a higher premium. But then—Community Life is a stock company and Star Mutual is a mutual company, which would cancel out the difference somewhat. None of which affects the problem, I suppose."

"No," Hendricks said. "The problem is where did she come up with the nearly nineteen hundred. Not to mention why she bought the insurance in the first place, and made Howard the beneficiary in the second place. Not to mention the question of who snatched, or who she ran away from and why."

"You think maybe she just ducked out?"

"Just a possibility. From the looks of her room, she was dragged out."

"That's your third piece of cake."

"Is it? That makes up for three murders. Two kidnappings to go. You came up with some good leads when you started the Parnet investigation. You went unerringly to the right spot, so to speak. If you were working on this Johnson thing, how would you go about it?"

"How do you manage to eat so much, and stay skinny?"

"That's your third piece of cake. How do you manage to eat so much and stay short?"

"I'd go to her place of employment. Except that I probably wouldn't because I've been there three times, and my welcome is wearing a little thin. That's one reason I turned the job down. At the place of employment, the girl at the switchboard, who is Sally Landis, now, would tell me...." He paused. "Know what Sally told me this morning? She wasn't surprised about Johnson being late to work, because last night was her date night. There wasn't any secret about those bridge dates."

"No, and they didn't break up early. But Johnson usually made it to work on time. Where would you go from the office?"

"I'd talk to the neighbors around Baker Street. Then I'd go

see her sister."

"Logical. Address?"

"I don't remember. Not too far from Johnson's place. She probably calls Johnson in to baby-sit."

"Shouldn't be hard to find. But that's what I mean. Nobody mentioned the sister. Next stop?"

"Brother killed in the war. Both parents probably dead, though she didn't mention her father. Next stop, former addresses. For thirty-five thousand dollars, we go back at least five years, and as much more as the circumstances seem to call for. On Betty Parnet we had to call in our Wisconsin office, because she'd only lived here for a year and a half."

"Johnson was been with Ronson and Wilcox for more than three years. They may have her earlier addresses."

"You have it then," Webber said. "The trick is to find someone who knows, and then to get that someone to talk. Friends, neighbors, acquaintances, fellow employees, employers. Does she have a police record?"

"No."

"You might check with the credit bureau, and find out how many bills she left unpaid while she was saving that nineteen hundred."

"I don't think that would get me anywhere, but I'll have somebody check. Anything else?"

"A good second look at Mr. Howard, and his affairs. Otherwise, no."

"And you're really out of this one?"

"Bob, if there was anything positive I could do to catch a murderer, or find Andrews and Johnson, I'd be off and running. But it isn't proper for me to nose around for the fun of it on my boss's time, and it isn't easy to nose around when you're in an unofficial position. If I come up with any ideas, you'll have them."

"Okay. I'll keep in touch with you. More coffee?"

"Half a cup. Thanks."

"I hate to go off and leave that much cake. I'll be worried

about you making yourself sick."

"Take a piece with you."

"Thanks. I will. This is going to worry my wife, though, when I pass up my midnight snack tonight."

"Here,—I'll get you some wax paper," Webber brought the paper from the kitchen, and made a neat package of the cake Hendricks sliced. "Coming to Frank's funeral?"

"I've been planning on it. If something doesn't break at the last minute, I'll be there."

"Let's hope we have a nice day."

Friday dawned out of a sickening drizzle. From his living-room window Webber looked down on the wet pavement and swore violently. The little angel seemed to enjoy every word of it. Frank would have enjoyed it too, Webber thought.

"Don't let it worry you, Ron. There's nothing like a rainy funeral to show a man who his true friends are."

Webber spent a miserable morning investigating small insurance applications. He went home at noon, his trouser legs soaked, his feet wet, and his clothing damp from perspiration generated by a hot raincoat. He took a shower, fixed a sandwich for himself, and rushed to type up his reports. He was back at the office at one, sifting through his next week's assignments, and picking out those he could do on Saturday. Boyd opened the door of his private office promptly at one-thirty.

"Want to ride with me?" he said.

"I'd better drive myself. We might need extra cars, and I promised to pick up Mrs. Mahoney."

"We'd better get started, then."

"I guess we'd better."

Along the way the rain changed from a drizzle to a downpour. Mrs. Mahoney filled the back seat with lamentations and Webber speeded up his windshield wipers and swore under his breath. Doris, riding beside him, told him she was glad she couldn't read lips.

The Clark Brothers were on hand with umbrellas, but it

still was a damp dash into the mortuary. Webber moved up front beside Mr. and Mrs. Boyd, and assumed the role of chief mourner. He cast startled glances over his shoulder at the crowd that filled the room and overflowed into the hallway.

"It isn't the real test yet, Ron. Watch them fade away when we start for the cemetery."

The Reverend Bruce Adkins, of the Carter City First Baptist Church, delivered the sermon. He was a young man, and Webber knew him casually and liked him.

"'For he brought nothing into this world, and it is certain we can carry nothing out.' The measure of life is the good which it leaves among us."

Webber listened with eyes closed while the Reverend Adkins's rich, powerful voice made the life of Frank Milford a thing of perhaps too much beauty.

"He'd better prop that good up with a little bad, Ron, or the whole thing's a going to collapse."

Doris sang some hymns, sincerely and beautifully. The ceremony concluded with a recording, by string orchestra, of Tchaikovsky's *None but the Lonely Heart*. Frank's favorite melody. Webber insisted on its inclusion, over the arched-eyebrow protests of the Reverend Adkins.

"You were right, Ron old boy. A man ought to be represented at his funeral by something more than his corpse."

The morticians had performed nobly. "Make him serious," Webber had told them. "Serious, but with a slight smile." They had almost succeeded. Webber looked up as he passed the casket, saw one of the elderly Brothers Clark looking anxiously, and gave him a firm nod of approval. The Brother Clark beamed happily.

Not until the procession was on its way to the cemetery did Webber realize that he had not seen Bob Hendricks among those present.

Sloshing through the grass in the rear corner of the cemetery, where he had purchased a lot for Frank, Webber's mind was on another interment which was taking place at a fancy, expensive location near the main entrance. As they passed he had caught a glimpse of William J. Howard, looking damp and grim after seeing his niece for the first and last time. Webber wondered if Howard wouldn't have enjoyed a loving niece, since his wife was dead and he had no children of his own. He needed young people and the sound of laughter in his life, to take his attention away from electric adding machines and bridge points, and he had passed up his last opportunity without really being aware of it. Ronson and Wilcox were among the thin crowd of mourners, along with their office girls. Webber recognized Sally, with her damp face buried in a damp handkerchief.

The Reverend Adkins mercifully made the graveside ceremony brief. Webber chauffeured Mrs. Mahoney home, and then drove Doris back to the office. He picked up his briefcase and started back to work, but his first stop was police headquarters, to see what had happened to Bob Hendricks.

The lieutenant was out. Webber wasted fifteen minutes waiting before he decided to move along. Hendricks caught up with him in the parking lot, and hauled him back inside, out of the rain.

"I came in the front as you were going out the back," he said.

"I missed you at the funeral."

"Sorry I couldn't make it. We've been busy." He slipped out of his raincoat, and dried his face on his sleeve. "We've got Morton."

"That's a good break. Did he talk?"

"His talking days are over. He was fished out of Round Lake this morning."

Webber said, "Oh." So another bright lead was punctured. He wondered if Falcone and his company had returned to the shabby Round Lake cottage. He wondered if Falcone had finally gotten around to doing something about the non-resident brigands.

"Drowned, I suppose," he said.

"Drowned with the help of a couple of stout whacks on the back of the head. Now figure that one if you can."

"He was hot, and this made him hotter. But why Round Lake? Why not Echo Lake?"

Carter City enjoyed the proximity of two lakes, but few people had so much as seen Echo Lake. Round Lake had sandy beaches, and a gently sloping bottom. It was highly popular, and ringed with cottages. Echo Lake was hidden in a heavily wooded sector, long and narrow, deep with a treacherous drop-off along its entire perimeter. Accessible only by private road, there were few cottages on Echo Lake, and those were the property of dedicated fishermen who preferred to pursue their prey in waters unmolested by racing pleasure boats, water skiers, and swimmers. A body dumped in the lonely waters of Echo Lake might drift unnoticed for months—or eternity.

"Simple," Hendricks said. "There are even better places than Echo Lake to hide a body. All they'd had to do was bury it off in the woods somewhere, or dump it in either lake weighted with a slab of concrete. They didn't, because they wanted us to find it. They made a clumsy effort to make it look like an accident. A stolen boat was floating upside down in the general area where the body was found. He had an empty wallet in his pocket, and one piece of identification carefully included. A driver's license in the name of Sam Morton, with a non-existent Chicago address. They hoped we'd take it for an accident, but either way they wanted to make certain we knew who we were getting."

"The wallet was supposed to have some money."

"That's what I think. Whoever gave Morton the final push couldn't see the sense of that stuff going to waste. But parties unknown have found out that Morton is the only definite suspect we have in this Parnet-Milford-Lamont-Andrews-Johnson business, so they're handing him over. We're supposed to joyfully announce that the murderer's evil ways have caught up with him, and close the case."

"How are you going to handle it?"

"Oh, we'll announce that we have the murderer. We know he was involved in the deal on the Parnet car, and he probably had a hand in running down Frank Milford and shooting Mrs. Lamont. We'll announce that, and then if I can scrape them up we'll put a few more men on the case."

"Anything else new?"

"The Andrews girl's mother received a ransom note. The poor woman has been sick, and this almost gave her a relapse."

"It's a red herring."

"Or maybe a crank. We're still checking on Morton. Parnet's neighbors identify him as the man who sold the car. A couple of the office girls at Ronson and Wilcox recognize him as a man who has been in a few times. Wilcox thinks he was after some political appointment—which one he can't remember because he gets a lot of callers like that. Ronson thinks he came in to sell something, but doesn't remember talking to him personally. William J. Howard claims he's never met the man."

"Maybe this will be a break for Marilyn Andrews. The name she was trying to think of was Morton, and if the man is dead there's no point in their holding her any longer."

"Could be, if she doesn't know a few other things, and if she's being held. As I said, there are a lot of good hiding places for a body. Where are you going?"

Webber paused in the doorway, and looked gloomily out into the drizzle. "Back to work."

CHAPTER ELEVEN

"Someone telephoned while I was cleaning," Mrs. Mahoney said. "So I answered the phone for you. He wouldn't leave a message, and he wouldn't tell me who he was."

"Odd," Webber said. "Did he say he'd call again?"

"I don't think so. I couldn't make out everything he said."

"There shouldn't be anything to worry about. If it was important, he'll call again."

Mrs. Mahoney wagged her finger. "I think it was that man that called himself Scarecrow. He used big words that didn't make sense."

"I'll call him," Webber said. "Thanks."

Webber dropped onto the sofa, and picked up the telephone book. "Doubt if I'll find a listing under 'Scarecrow,' but Falcone should know where he is, or be able to get a message to him. Falcone...."

He tossed the telephone book aside. Obviously it would be easier to reach Scarecrow if he knew his name. He picked up the telephone, and on the third try he located Bob Hendricks.

"A couple of days ago, you said something about Falcone's right-hand man. What was his name?"

"You mean Pronk?"

"Pronk. That was it. Thanks."

"What do you have up your sleeve now?"

"Not a thing," Webber said. "My arms are bare to the shoulders."

He called Nick Falcone's city residence. A deeply masculine

voice answered.

"I'd like to speak with Mr. Pronk."

The voice laughed coarsely. "*Mister* Pronk ain't in."

"Could you get a message to him?"

"Sooner or later."

"This is Ron Webber. Tell him I'll be home all evening."

"That sounds like real big news. Sure—I'll pass it along."

"Thanks."

Webber hung up, and indulged in some coarse laughter of his own. He'd committed himself to staying in all evening, which meant that he'd have to fix his own supper. And his larder was bare. He went down to see if he could borrow some wieners from Mrs. Mahoney, and she promptly invited him to partake of one of her inimitable meals.

And he had to decline, because from her apartment he wouldn't be able to hear his telephone. Scarecrow did not call, and by midnight he had thought of several names for the gentleman gangster, none of them complimentary.

In the morning he called Falcone's residence again. The answering voice was not the same, but very similar. "Yeah—message for Pronk from Ron Webber. We didn't give it to Pronk 'cause he didn't show. You want us to tell him now you'll be home all morning?"

"No," Webber said. "Tell him he'll just have to trust to luck."

"Pronk'll like that. He's real lucky."

"I bet," Webber said.

He lined up his Saturday morning investigations, and worked north from the center of town. He was almost out to the suburbs with a good two hours of work behind him when a patrol car picked him up. It closed on him fast, and he watched it in the rear-view mirror with a momentary feeling of panic. What had he done? Improper left turn? Excessive speed?

He knew he hadn't done anything wrong, and it was with a sense of outraged innocence that he obeyed the signal and pulled over.

The patrol car stopped abreast of him, and the officer slid

over and rolled down the window. "Ron Webber?"

"That's right."

"You're needed at Provincial Hospital. I'll lead."

Webber reacted slowly. Providence Hospital. "You mean the Old Man...," he began, but the patrol car had already pulled away. He jammed down the accelerator, and followed it.

"Just like him," he muttered. "Lectured everyone else on playing it safe, and then he tries to make a one-man war out of it. Wonder how many fingers he lost this time."

He remembered those other times vividly. His mother had been alive, then. She'd taken one look and fainted when the Old Man had come home with his face bandaged up, and when he'd lost the finger she had kicked up a scene and tried to make him find another job. His parents had loved each other, but their marriage hadn't been a particularly happy one. His mother worried too much. She hadn't been cut out to be a policeman's wife.

And the Old Man's favorite insult was to tell Webber he took after his mother.

The patrol car kept a moderate, steady pace through the Saturday morning traffic, using the siren only at intersections. Webber kept doggedly behind it. Providence Hospital. Those other times they hadn't known about it until the Old Man walked in, jauntily attempting to conceal his bandages. There hadn't been any mad dashes to the hospital, or even a telephone call. So this time it would be different. This time it wouldn't be a scarred cheek or a missing finger.

He flipped on the car radio, hoping for a spot news bulletin. Either he had already missed it, or what had happened wasn't officially news. He wove his way through traffic after the patrol car, and the radio played jazzy music.

At the hospital he left his car under a sign that warned, "Ambulances—emergency only," and outdistanced the officer by ten feet to reach the door. The officer caught him at the elevator.

"Sixth floor," he said

"What happened?"

"Don't know. They said to bring you. I brought you."

The elevator hunched its way upwards in a maddening crawl. Of all the places in the world that ought to have a good elevator service, Webber thought, a hospital should be one. But he stood crowded between a woman in a wheel chair and a man on a stretcher, and watched the man's face contort with pain each time the elevator jerked.

The sixth floor. The officer stopped to question a nurse, and she pointed down the corridor before he opened his mouth. They rounded a corner, and found a bored sheriff's deputy tilted back in a chair beside a door. He looked the two of them over, and said without interest, "Webber, I suppose. You can leave him."

"With pleasure," the officer said. "Where's Murphy?"

"Talking with the doctor. Why?"

"Just thought I'd ask. I'll be seeing you." He walked away.

"If it isn't too much to ask," Webber said, "what happened?"

"Friend of yours got himself shot. Guy named Pronk."

Webber took a deep breath, and sank back against the wall. "I see. Is he hurt badly?"

"Five bullets in him. He isn't hurt good. And he won't talk to anyone but you. So we had you picked up."

The doctor came quietly down the corridor, with Sheriff Murphy striding behind him. Murphy jarred Webber with a slap on the back, punched at his shoulder, and jerked a thumb at the door. "Pal of yours, eh? How come?"

"Beats me. I've met him exactly once. Does Hendricks know about this?"

"Hendricks?" Murphy's eyes narrowed. "Would this have something to do with the murders?"

"I'll give you small odds that it does. Say a hundred to one."

Murphy whistled. "I'd better call Bob." He started away, turned back abruptly. "Look—when the doctor lets you in, there's two things I want. Who did it, and where did it happen. Got that? Who and where. If you can get them, why and how that's okay too. Don't leave before I get back." He rushed off.

The deputy got out a knife, and solemnly went to work on his fingernails.

"About four A.M. he was driving back towards Carter City. Down in the vicinity of Round Lake he passed out, and ran off the road. Luckily for him, one of our cars was right behind him, and they rushed him in. He must be a hell of a tough guy. Nobody knows how far he drove with those holes unplugged, but he damn near bled to death. And we can't get very far on the thing until we know where it happened." The doctor appeared in the doorway, frostily professional. "Mr. Webber?"

"Yes," Webber said.

"I can give you three minutes. And I intend to be present."

Webber smiled. "I assure you that I have no objection."

"Mr. Pronk does," the doctor said shortly.

Webber followed him into the room.

Scarecrow lay with his eyes closed, looking much too long for the bed. His gaunt face approximated the shade of the white bandage that hid the top of his head. He was receiving another transfusion, and a nurse was bending over him anxiously.

"How is he?" Webber asked the doctor.

"Five bullets," the doctor said. "And that doesn't count the one that creased his head. But he'll live."

Scarecrow opened his eyes. His lips formed the words, "Master Webber." Webber bent over him. "Get them out of here," Scarecrow whispered.

Webber shook his head. "They're saving your life, chump. Be nice to them."

A frown creased his forehead. Frustration, pain, weariness were etched on his face. His lips moved again. The whisper was barely audible.

"Echo Lake. West side. Cottage."

"I understand," Webber said.

"Cottage. Belongs to—Wilcox."

"Apartment. 384 Baker. Number three."

"I understand."

"The girl. She's...." He broke off, and swallowed painfully.

"One place or the other?" Webber suggested.

The nod was just perceptible.

"Do you know which girl—Johnson or Andrews?"

The lips formed the word. "No."

"The sheriff would like to know who shot you, and where."

Scarecrow stirred, and drew upon some mysterious reserve of strength. The whisper was stronger. "Can't have the police busting in. Girl's alive. They'd have time—they might—"

"I understand. The police might handle the apartment, but there'd be lookouts at the lake. Maybe it was a lookout that spotted you."

A wisp of a smile touched his lips. "Maybe."

The doctor said firmly, "That's enough, Mr. Webber."

"What shall I tell the sheriff?" Webber said. "He wants to know who and where."

The whisper was scornful. "I'll give the matter—due consideration."

"Right. I thank you, and I'll see what can be done." He gripped Scarecrow's limp hand and turned away. He paused before he opened the door. "You know something? You remind me of an angel I know." As Scarecrow winced, he added, "This angel doesn't wear a badge."

Sheriff Murphy grabbed Webber as he came out of the room. "What'd he say?"

"He says he'll think it over."

"I don't buy that. You were in there long enough to collaborate on a book. If you think you can hold out on me, and let your old man...."

The doctor appeared in the doorway. As the sheriff stepped forward, he said coldly, "No more visitors."

"You were there, Doc. What'd they talk about."

"I never eavesdrop on private conversations."

They watched the doctor walk away. The sheriff said, "Doesn't he want us to find out who did it? Don't you?"

"Was Scarecrow—I mean Pronk—carrying a gun?"

"He never does. Too smart, I suppose. He's always being

picked up by somebody on suspicion of something or other. We'd have him on a concealed weapons charge fifty times a year, if he did."

"Look—I concede that you have a kind of priority on this thing, since you found him, and whatever happened must have happened outside the city limits. Go back to your office—"

The sheriff stiffened. "Just who do you think you are?"

"—go back to your office and wait for a phone call from me. The city police ought to be in on it too, but I'll leave that up to you."

"Hendricks is on his way over."

"Then I'd better get out of here. I'll call you at your office."

"The sheriff glared angrily. "I'll be there. And it better be good."

Hendricks was arriving as Webber drove away. He leaped out of his car and waved frantically, and Webber pretended not to see him. He looked back as he turned, and saw Hendricks and Sheriff Murphy talking in the parking lot. Hendricks's arms were still waving.

Webber drove three blocks, turned, and parked on a side street. Moments later the Sheriff's official car flashed by, with Hendricks in close pursuit.

"Naughty," Webber murmured. "Thirty miles an hour over the speed limit."

He leaned back and closed his eyes, and lost himself in thought.

Attorney James Wilcox owned a cottage on Echo Lake. That much wasn't surprising. Despite his bulk, Wilcox looked the rugged, outdoor type. He probably liked to fish, so he owned an Echo Lake cottage.

Echo Lake cottages were few and widely separated. If they were built back more than fifty feet from the lake, they were hidden in the trees. Webber had been fishing in Echo Lake once, with the Old Man, as a guest of somebody or other. He hadn't liked the place. But that had been years before, when he was a kid.

Scarecrow had been found on Ridge Road, near Round Lake. Ridge Road grazed Round Lake, but Echo Lake was ten miles west. To reach Echo Lake it was necessary to drive south on Ridge Road as far as Round Lake, turn west on a county road that wound its way through light woods and scraggly pastures, and finally turn off the county road onto a private road to reach the lake proper. The private road would rarely be more than a couple of tire tracks through thick woods.

Ditto in reverse for the return journey. Scarecrow, he thought, had made that return journey with his life oozing steadily away. He had no place to turn for help until he got back to Ridge Road, and by then he would have been too far gone to act rationally.

Had Scarecrow been shot in the woods and left for dead? Or had he eluded his pursuers in a wild chase and kept going in spite of his wounds? Webber wondered if Scarecrow's car showed signs of a gun battle. More likely, he had hidden his car and approached the lake on foot. The entire fracas would have taken place under cover of darkness, and Scarecrow would have staggered to safety through the dark woods, found his car, and driven until he lost consciousness.

A cottage on Echo Lake made an ideal hiding place for anyone or anything. There was also the apartment in town to consider. The address alone was suggestive. 384 Baker. It could hardly be coincidence that Ruth Johnson had lived at 387.

Webber drove back up town, to the National Credit Company office. Doris was just leaving, and Webber solemnly promised to lock the door when he left, and put out the cat if he found any around.

The city directory informed him that four families lived at 384 Baker. The names meant nothing. The directory was nearly a year old, and in that time all four families could have moved.

The telephone directory, which was six months old, listed the same four names. "But one apartment must have changed hands since then," Webber thought. "Number three."

He went to the company files, and checked the names on his list. A year before, a Mrs. Sarah Wilson, 384 Baker, Apartment

One, had applied for a life insurance policy. She had lived for nine years at that address. Webber thought it likely that she still lived there. He took an inspection form, gave it a current date, and filled in the name and relevant statistics of Mrs. Sarah Wilson. He prepared similar forms for Betty Parnet and Ruth Johnson.

He called Sheriff Murphy. "I just wanted to be sure you were in your office," he said.

"Webber, I don't like to play games. What are you up to?"

"I'll be calling you again. Say, within half an hour. Is Hendricks there?"

"He is."

"I think half-a-dozen men could handle this, but you may want more, just to be safe. Say ten men. Have them ready when I call back."

He hung up.

Webber parked his car on Langly Street, and walked around the corner to Baker, moving slowly from door to door, carrying his briefcase. He rang no doorbells, but he put on his best imitation of a plodding door-to-door salesman, and he looked the neighborhood over carefully. At 384 he learned that the Wilson family was still in residence, and that the building's front door was not kept locked. He reached the end of the block, turned, and walked down the street to a filling station to telephone.

"How long will it take you to get to Baker Street?" he asked the sheriff.

"Three minutes," Murphy said.

"Driving at moderate speeds, and without sirens. Can you make it in ten minutes?"

"Easy."

Webber glanced at his watch. "All right," he said. "I have twenty after twelve. In exactly ten minutes I'm going to be knocking at the door of Apartment Three, 384 Baker. Got that?"

"Apartment Three, 384 Baker. We'll be there."

"You will not!" Webber snapped. "You're to come quietly,

park over on Langly, and walk to the house. Cover it front and back, and do it without arousing the neighborhood. I want ten uninterrupted minutes there. If you start playing cops and robbers before twenty to one, I'll spit in your face."

"Okay. We come quietly, cover the place, and at twenty to one we'll be at the door of Apartment Three."

"Check. I'll be seeing you." He hung up and added, "I hope."

He walked quickly up the steps of 384 Baker. In the first floor hallway he paused to get his clipboard in order. He placed the Betty Parnet form on top, the Ruth Johnson form second, and the fake Sarah Wilson form third. Below them came the forms for a dozen new cases that had been assigned to him the day before.

At twenty-nine minutes after twelve, he boldly climbed the stairs and knocked on the door of apartment number three.

The door opened a crack. A masculine voice growled, "Yeah?"

"How do you do," Webber said brightly. "I'd like to ask you some questions, if you don't mind."

The crack widened, and a squat, heavily built man appeared in the opening. "How's that?"

Webber shifted the clipboard. He did not exactly hold it under the man's nose, but he made certain that it wouldn't be over-looked. "Just a few simple questions," he said. "There's a Mrs. Sarah Wilson who lives on the first floor. Do you know her?"

"What's this all about?" His eyes were on the clipboard, on the form that listed the name and vital statistics of Betty Parnet.

"Do you know Mrs. Sarah Wilson?"

The door swung open. The man's hands shot out, gripped Webber's shoulders, and jerked him through the door. As the door slammed something struck the back of his head. It was a glancing blow, but he reeled dizzily, and before he quite got his balance a hand shoved him to the floor. He sat there stupidly, too dazed to protest.

Two men stood looking down at him and one of them, the one he'd met at the door, was indifferently holding a stubby-looking revolver. The other one had picked up the clipboard and was leafing through the forms.

Webber started to get up, and changed his mind when the man with the gun ordered him to stay where he was. The man with the clipboard pointed it at him.

"Talk."

"About what?"

"What's your line?"

"Insurance investigator."

He leafed through the forms again. "What do you know about Betty Parnet?"

Webber sensed the tension in the room. The gun pointed unwaveringly. He assumed what he hoped was an innocent expression. "Who is Betty Parnet?"

The clipboard was thrust under his nose.

"Oh," Webber said. "She's some dame what's applied for an insurance policy. I haven't gotten around to her yet."

"And Ruth Johnson?"

Webber looked at the form. "Likewise."

The man with the gun took a step forward. "I oughta bust you in the teeth."

The other man shook his head. "Johnson did. I heard about it. There was some kind of angle." He turned to Webber. "You're here checking on this Mrs. Wilson?"

"That's right."

"And this is the way you investigate? Snooping around the neighbors?"

"We make inquiries of neighbors," Webber said stiffly. "We also check with employers, and fellow employees and anyone who may be able to give accurate and impartial information."

"And these other people—" he waved the clipboard "—they've all applied for insurance so you're investigating them?"

"As fast as I can get around to them, yes. I'm running behind schedule."

"So you have to work Saturday," Clipboard said. "Isn't that just too bad."

Webber sat uncomfortable on the floor, and sneaked a glance at his watch. Five minutes had gone by since he had knocked at the door. The next five minutes, he thought, might be the longest he'd ever experienced.

Clipboard was going through the forms again. "I think," he announced finally, "that you made a bad mistake, Mike. The guy just might be legit."

Mike shrugged, and gestured absently with the gun. "He just might not, too."

"Either way, we're stuck with him. He might be legit, but he's probably not stupid. Sooner or later he'll go howling to the cops. The boss'll want him iced until this is finished."

"We'll have to wait 'til tonight."

"Of course. After dark."

"What's your name, fellow?" Mike said.

"Would it hurt your feelings if I told you it was none of your business?"

"Take his wallet," Mike said. "I don't want to hurt his feelings."

Webber sat helplessly while his was wallet was being filched. There was a long glance at the identification, and then a longer glance at Webber. "Well!"

"Who is he?" Mike asked.

"Ronald Webber, Junior."

"Webber! Then he's the one...."

"Yeah. He's legit all right. That's what he is—an insurance investigator."

"I don't like the looks of this. Does he work by himself?"

"I'll take a look."

Webber took a deep breath as Clipboard crossed warily to the window. "Nobody in sight," he announced.

"Think we ought to let the boss know?"

They retired to the far corner of the room, and engaged in a whispered discussion. Mike kept his eyes and his gun on Webber.

Webber looked again at his watch. Two minutes.

"It doesn't make any difference," Clipboard said aloud. "We're stuck with him."

"You can't telephone until...."

There were some more whispers, and some ugly glances in Webber's direction. Thirty seconds to go.

The knock on the door rattled the furniture across the room. "Open up," a voice called. "Police. You have five seconds to get this door open. One, two, three...."

They smashed in the door on the first rush. Mike was standing with mouth agape, his gun pointing midway between Webber and the door. He dropped it, and slowly raised his hands. Clipboard made a rush for the back room, and Sheriff Murphy flattened him with one punch. Webber relaxed, but only for a moment. The third person through the door was the Old Man.

He jerked Webber to his feet. "Of all the idiotic things to do—you deserve a whipping, and I'm just the man to give it to you. With a hairbrush. Thought you hadn't had enough heroics this week, I suppose. You can't say you were just doing your job on this one. You deliberately withheld information from the police so you could walk in here and get yourself messed up in it. You could have gotten some of my men, or Murphy's men, killed. They couldn't handle this the way it should be handled. They had to come busting in here to rescue you. With all you know about police procedure, I thought you had the brains...."

He had more to say, and he said it. He towered over Webber; fists clenched, face a flaming red, and spouted invective. Hendricks stood nearby, shifting his feet at brief intervals, and looking embarrassedly in the direction of the kitchen. Webber waited, and kept his mouth shut. Even the Old Man had to run down eventually, and he did, and turned on his heel, and walked away.

Mike and Clipboard—minus the clipboard—were hustled away. The Old Man and Murphy started their men on the apartment. Hendricks turned to Webber.

"It really wasn't very bright, Ron. Not what you'd call necessary. What were you trying to do?"

"Just what I did," Webber said.

"Were you trying to make the capture single-handed? That isn't like you. You got in the way, you know."

"Look," Webber said. "What are you going to do with those two? What's the charge? Oh, I know Mike had a gun, and maybe the other one was armed. Maybe they keep sawed-off shotguns under the bed. I'm betting you won't find anything else of interest. They held a gun on an insurance investigator, but what else have you got?"

Hendricks looked at him blankly. "I thought Pronk...."

"Maybe Mike's gun shot Pronk. I doubt it. I doubt if you can prove they had anything to do with that. It certainly didn't happen here. You don't have a gun battle on Baker Street with no one noticing, and if you did, how did Pronk get down to Round Lake?"

"I hadn't thought about it," Hendricks admitted. "It happened so fast, you know, and we tore over here—what is the pitch?"

"Supposing I'd given you the word, and kept out of it. A couple of out-of-town crooks holed up in an apartment on Baker Street. Probably they have records. Maybe they're wanted somewhere. So you pick them up, and maybe you have a weapons charge or maybe you haven't. And of course they say they're in Carter City to visit some old friends, and beyond that they won't talk. What have you got?"

"Not much," Hendricks admitted.

"All right. I played it my way. Here's the story." He described his adventure with the clipboard, and the reactions of the two men. Hendricks examined the forms, and shook his head.

"I apologize. I apologize for the Old Man, too, because he won't."

"You don't have to guess. You know, now, that they're connected with the Parnet case, and you know you can crack this thing if they talk. Making them talk is up to you."

Hendricks grabbed Webber's hand. "I'll make them talk."

The Old Man stormed back into the room, saw Webber, and halted. "You still here?"

Webber grinned. "As a witness."

"Hell of a witness you'd make. Hendricks, you've been too chummy with this idiot, and it's giving him ideas about playing policeman. I want it stopped. I don't want you or anyone else discussing police cases with him. Is that clear?"

"He had the right idea on this one," Hendricks said.

"Nuts! He hasn't had a right idea since he was seven years old. That's a direct order. I want it posted, and all personnel notified. If I hear of any man discussing a police case with my son, he'll be looking a long time for his next promotion. Is that clear?"

Webber took the clipboard from Hendricks, and picked up his briefcase. A deputy sheriff returned his wallet.

"He's cooperated pretty well," Hendricks was saying.

"Nuts!" the Old Man said. "You mean you've cooperated with him. I want it stopped.

Anger blinded Webber. The Old Man had always been a square shooter, patient when a man faltered, and quick with praise when he succeeded. He ran the police department with an iron hand, but he ran it fairly. No man could accuse him of being unjust.

No man except his own son.

He managed to steer a steady course for the door, where he turned to have the last word. "Cooperation is a two-way street, gentlemen. It looks as if I'll have to solve this Parnet business myself."

He listened carefully as he went down the stairs. From the room above came nothing but silence.

CHAPTER TWELVE

Webber finished his hamburger, pushed the plate aside, and reached for the cup of coffee. "Good sandwich," he said. "Better fix me another one."

The counter man nodded. From the refrigerator he took the thick oval of meat, expertly slapped it onto the grill, and whipped off the square of wax paper. "Our hamburgers got meat in," he said. "Not every place can make that statement."

It was well past the lunch hour, and Webber had the diner to himself. From his seat at the counter he could see Ridge Road, and beyond it, Round Lake. The lake was choppy under an overcast sky. There was the fresh scent of threatening rain in the air. Ridge Road traffic hummed past fitfully.

Webber had driven directly out Ridge Road from the address on Baker Street. He had driven this far, and then he had stopped to eat.

Item: Marilyn Andrews or Ruth Johnson was being held at a cottage on Echo Lake

Item: The cottage was guarded formidably. Scarecrow had six bullet wounds to prove it.

The first problem, as Webber saw it, was not to catch a murderer, but to get the girl out of there. Scarecrow thought that a mass rescue attempt would result in the death of the girl. If her captors considered her dangerous, he was probably right.

What could Webber do about it?

The Old Man was scratched. Eliminated. Completely out of it. Echo Lake was outside his territory, and even if it weren't

Webber was donating no more leads to the city police. He could tip off the sheriff and let him handle it. And the sheriff would call out all his deputies and get some help from the state police, and they would head through the woods about as unobtrusively as a herd of elephants, and shoot their way in. They would get the girl, all right. Dead or alive.

He realized that he hadn't answered his question. What could Webber do about it?

He could collect information. He was a trained investigator, and an expert at talking with people and finding out what they knew. Unfortunately, no one would know very much about a cottage on Echo Lake.

He could reconnoiter the place, and see for himself what could be done. This would be rash to the point of stupidity. Scarecrow had probably been attempting no more than that.

He could wait. Perhaps Hendricks would induce his two captives to talk, and break the case wide open. He doubted this. The police had no evidence, and the men from Baker Street would not be easily bluffed.

He was certain of only one thing—he would have to do something himself. Perhaps the police could handle the situation properly, perhaps not. But he had promised the Old Man. It was a promise he meant to keep.

"Know anything about Echo Lake?" Webber asked.

The counter man scooped up Webber's hamburger deftly, transferred the meat to a bun, and slid the plate across the counter. "They say the fish are almost as big as the mosquitoes."

The answer was a casual shake of the head. "It's all private around there. Either you gotta know somebody, or you gotta trespass. And they say the bank's no good to fish from in most places—just a mess of brush. Friend of mine took a boat down there once and when he got it in the water the owner of the place popped out from behind a tree and charged him ten bucks. No, I like my lakes civilized. Maybe the fish aren't as big, but neither are the mosquitoes."

"Do you know anyone who does know his way around Echo

Lake?"

"Bert would. Bert Latham. He runs the service station down yonder.

"Thanks," Webber said. "I'll look him up."

The sign said, "Latham's Round Lake Service." Webber asked for Bert Latham, and the young attendant jerked a thumb at the station. Webber found the proprietor leaning back in a chair, feet on his desk, puffing steadily on a corncob pipe. Healthy-looking, robust, he could have passed for forty with a hat on. Without the hat, his grey hair made him sixty-five.

"Know Echo Lake like my own back yard," he told Webber. "Matter of fact, it kind of is my back yard. Got a cottage there myself, you know. Wonderful place. Spend most of my spare time there, in the summer. I'd be over there today if it wasn't threatening rain. It's not fished like it used to be, and the fish get bigger every year. Most of the men who own cottages there are getting on in years and they don't use them much. I used to do a pretty good bait business right here at the station. They'd order it by phone, and pick it up on their way out to the lake. But some of them don't show up once a summer, now. You figuring on buying a place?"

"I'm an insurance investigator," Webber said.

"You don't say." He half turned, and looked at Webber respectfully. "Didn't know there was anything around Echo Lake that was worth insuring. None of them cottages are fancy. Just places to sleep and cook fish. But I suppose some of those fellows would insure anything if they thought there was a chance of collecting."

"This cottage I'm interested in belongs to a man named Wilcox."

"Know Jim well. Used to do a lot of fishing with him, years ago. Bet it's been a couple of years since he's wet a line, though. He stops off, sometimes, when he's down this way, and we talk about the ones that got away. Them were the days. A man doesn't realize what it's like to only be young once, until he's old. You looking for Jim's cottage?"

"If you could direct me, I'd appreciate it."

"Isn't easy to find anything, on Echo Lake. All private property around there, you know. Well, let's see. This road right here is Heyers Road. They call it something else on the county maps, but we always called it Heyers Road, because old man Heyers used to have a farm out that way. Heyers Road runs south of Echo Lake, right straight through to the state line, and if you don't want to go there you better watch your turns."

"Jim's place is on the west side of the lake. I could give you the names of the cross roads, but it wouldn't help you, 'cause there aren't any signs back there, anyway. The one you want to remember is Frost Road. There isn't any sign there, either, but you can't miss it because it dead-ends on Heyers Road. Comes in from the south, and can't go any further on account of the lake. It's all woods on the north side of the road, and Frost Road comes in from the south. Then you turn north on the first road after that. Got it?"

"Frost Road dead ends on Heyers Road, and I turn north on the next cross road."

"Right. Kind of tricky, because you never catch a glimpse of the lake. Lots of woods there and the only way to get to the lake is on private roads, if you want to call them roads. Now let me think."

He closed his eyes and mumbled to himself, counting on his fingers. It'll be the seventh turn-off," he announced finally. "Better drive slow, because some of them may be grown over and hard to see. But the seventh turn-off after you turn north will take you to Jim's cottage. Follow it straight in. That was the original road, and some of them that built cottages later made branches off his road so they wouldn't have so far to go. Think you can find it?"

"Sure, I can find it," Webber said. "Many thanks."

He returned to his car, but he did not drive away immediately. Instead, he wrote a letter to Sheriff Murphy. Failure wasn't out of the question—it almost seemed probable. If he did fail, he owed it to the girl, whoever she was, to let someone else know.

He sealed the letter in an envelope, and took it in to Bert Latham. "How late are you open?" he asked.

"Midnight."

"If I'm not back by ten o'clock, I'd like to have you call Sheriff Murphy, and read this to him."

Latham did not reach for the envelope. He smoked silently for a few minutes, his eyes on Webber. "You really an insurance investigator?"

Webber nodded.

Latham took the envelope, and carefully stowed it away in an inside pocket. "Quite a few times lately I seen strangers heading down towards the lake. And Pete Young told me last night he heard shooting over on the west side. Sure, I'll call the sheriff. Ten o'clock you say?"

"Ten o'clock. Don't open it before then." Webber smiled as he opened the door. "I'll be seeing you."

The private roads were no more than dim pairs of car tracks curving back into the woods. The only one that showed signs of recent use was number five, and Webber had to check twice to find the two he had overlooked. So the well-used tracks would be the ones that led to the Wilcox cottage.

Webber was too much a city boy to feel at home in the country, but it did not take knowledge of woodcraft to see that the trees were thick and the undergrowth was a tangled mess. There could be no such thing as a casual stroll through that miniature wilderness. To make matters worse, the sky had darkened ominously. Lightning flashed in the distance, and thunder rumbled faintly. Webber studied the sky with the practiced eye of one who had to get around in all kinds of weather, and decided that it would rain before evening.

A short distance beyond the Wilcox road, he backed his car off the road and into the woods. He got out and kicked his tire tracks into the dirt, and looked around. The woods held that curious before-the-storm stillness. There were no human sounds. The narrow county road humped its way over a flimsy bridge and disappeared around a curve. Probably no more than half-dozen cars had used the road since yesterday's rain. Perhaps no more than two or three.

Webber contemplated the quiet with a twinge of nervousness. "A good hiding place," he told himself.

He went back to his car, and emptied his pockets into the glove compartment. The men in the Baker Street apartment had recognized his name immediately, and such undeserved fame could be embarrassing. If he were captured, he'd have a chance of bluffing his way out of it if they did not know who he was. He wouldn't let his own identification give him away a second time.

He locked the car, and hid the keys under the hood. Carrying only a plastic raincoat that folded to pocket size, he walked boldly down the private road towards the Wilcox cottage.

The tracks wound in and out among the trees, veering suddenly to one side, and straightening out just as unexpectedly. He had no idea how far it was to the lake, but he was gambling that any sentries would be posted near the cottage.

When he had walked about a quarter of a mile along the winding trail, he paused and reluctantly considered the woods. Perhaps it was time for a more cautious approach. Perhaps he had been lucky to come so far without being seen. There was no sense in pressing his luck.

Suddenly he heard the car. He dove for the undergrowth, and put precious yards between himself and the road. It had come surprisingly close without his hearing it, but the motor was not running loudly, and the trees would muffle some of the sound. It bounced along the rough road in second gear, and passed his hiding place, the driver obviously proceeding slowly, and with extreme caution.

Webber remained crouching, although he knew that he could not be seen from the road. As the first car's motor died away, he heard a second approaching.

"Traffic is too heavy," he muttered.

Reluctant to waste more time, he pushed forward through

the woods. Every step was a painful struggle. Branches raked against him, and he had already been made painfully aware of the oversized mosquitoes.

He broke through suddenly into a small clearing. It was only a few feet across and quite without interest except for the dead rabbit that lay in the center. The rabbit had been shot. Webber felt a flash of disgust as he visualized a big-city gunman taking a quick, joking shot at a rabbit through a car window, and then not being interested enough to see what happened to it.

"Someone handles a gun well," he thought.

He heard another car coming, this time from the opposite direction. He waited in the clearing until it had passed, and then he moved on. His progress was so slow and tortuous that he was tempted to return to the road and take his chances. The memory of Scarecrow, white and bandaged on the hospital bed, blunted the temptation.

He pushed on, trying to walk in a straight line, and suddenly he was back on the road again. It had taken a sharp curve to the north, and now it ran straight for fifty yards. He could see the lake ahead, and the cottage.

He approached cautiously, and studied it. It was a bleak, frame affair, much molested by time. Its white paint had peeled off in large patches. An effort at landscaping had been made in the past, with the only result being some evergreen shrubs grown to monstrous size. The small clearing around the cottage was wildly overgrown with tall weeds. Webber looked carefully for a car and saw none.

"Two came in," he told himself, "and one went out. What gives?"

He heard the cottage door bang, waited, and saw no one.

Moving stealthily, keeping under cover, he edged his way around the clearing. A window was up at the back of the cottage, and a faded, ragged curtain flapped in the breeze. By the open porch was a small pile of tin cans—recently opened cans, still untouched by rust.

"Someone living there," Webber thought, "and they're home.

Now what?"

He wondered if he dared risk an attempt to look through the window. Probably not, from this side. The clearing was wider here. Perhaps from the other side....

He worked his way back to the road, and he was ten feet from the man before he saw him. Blond, nattily attired in a checkered suit, he grinned evilly as he covered Webber with a revolver.

"Up," he ordered. "All the way up."

Webber held his arms straight up, and said calmly, "Do you have a permit to carry that gun?"

The gunman's jaw sagged slightly. He circled around behind Webber, patted him expertly, and satisfied himself that Webber was unarmed. Then he shooed Webber down the road towards the cottage.

"Nice to find the guilty party so easily," Webber said. "I thought you might give us a good chase."

The gunman halted. "What was that?"

"I said it's nice...."

"Who are you anyway?"

Webber had all the time he was stumbling through the woods to figure out an answer to that question. "Game Warden," he said. The gunman's face assumed a stupefied expression. "There's been some hunting going on through here. People reported they heard shots last night, and I found a dead rabbit on my way in here. Better put away your gun, and pay your fine, and forget it. Interfering with a game warden in the performance of his duty carries a heavy penalty."

"I haven't been doing any hunting," the gunman snapped. "And you don't look like a game warden."

Webber, with his hands still erect, shrugged. "You don't look like a hunter. But there it is. You have a gun, and I have a dead rabbit. If you didn't do it, who did?"

The gunman fell silent.

"Better come quietly," Webber suggested. "If the others come up and see you holding a gun on me, they might get the wrong idea."

The gunman stole quick side-glances at the woods. "What others?"

"There are six of us covering this territory. As I said, there was a lot of shooting around here last night. Didn't you hear it? Or were you doing it?"

The gunman gestured towards the cottage. "Come on," he said. But he was no longer pointing the gun directly at Webber.

He halted Webber at the side of the house, and walked around to the porch. "Says he's a game warden," he announced. "Says a lot of shooting was reported around here last night, and there are six of them snooping around, now. Says he found a dead rabbit. He wants to know who shot it."

The answer was a dry chuckle. "Nuts. Tell him we don't shoot rabbits unless they attack us. We only have guns to protect us from burglars."

"Should I tell him to beat it? A game warden...."

The voice dropped. There was an involved, two-way conversation in whispers. "I suppose," the second voice said.

A face peered around the edge of the house, glanced at Webber, stared. It was an ugly face, crowned with a shining bald head. A hand snapped into view, with a deadly-looking .45 automatic. "I'll be damned!"

Webber knew in that instant that his well-conducted bluff was demolished. He had last seen that particular face in a blue sedan, of unpleasant memories, just before a .45 had messed up his car. He had seen it only vaguely and he probably couldn't have picked its owner out of a police lineup, but the facial expression, combined with the automatic, made his identification positive.

"Game warden, eh? That's a hot one. This guy's no game warden, you idiot. This is that insurance investigator, Webber!"

He vaulted over the railing. Both guns were trained on Webber, now, and he knew that the trigger fingers were not relaxed.

Gunman number two repeated the patting operation, somewhat more roughly. Then he went through Webber's pockets.

He stepped back, obviously puzzled.

"Don't game wardens carry any identification at all? Pains me to see a man so broke he doesn't even have a wallet. Take him inside."

The gun jabbed Webber's back. He rounded the house, and climbed the two rickety steps to the porch. He stepped around two folding chairs, and moved on into the cottage.

There was a battered table in the center of the room, and two unpainted but very dirty chairs. At one time there had been linoleum on the floor, but only a few oddly shaped pieces remained. A small hand pump stood by the sink. In the far corner was a bulky icebox. There were two doors, one opening into a small bathroom. The other door was closed.

Webber waited with his hands over his head. The first gunman was not completely at ease about the situation. "He said there was six of them. Suppose they make trouble?"

"That's his worry. We got our orders. We got a lookout on the road, Webber. I don't know how you missed him, but a mob wouldn't, and if there's any trouble our orders are to shoot the girl and clear out. If it comes to that, you get it along with the girl. Better behave yourself."

The first gunman stepped forward to the closed door, shot a bolt back, and gestured. "Move."

Webber moved through the door, and into the bedroom. The girl was sitting on the opposite side of the room, facing the door. She had a magazine on her lap, and a stack of magazines on the floor beside her. It was Marilyn Andrews.

The flowered dress was soiled and wrinkled. Her face looked wan, her eyes tired, but she seemed unharmed. She gave him a shy smile that was more sympathetic than cheerful.

"Company, dearie," the gunman said. He kicked a chair into the room, and placed it in the corner. "Sit," he said. Webber sat.

"Stay put. If you take one step away from that chair, I'll tie you up and roll you under the bed."

He went out, and bolted the door behind him. His footsteps crossed the next room, and the screen door banged. Webber spoke bitterly. "Fine rescue expedition I am. Are you restricted to your chair?"

She nodded. "Even when they have the door closed, they try to see what I'm doing. I've seen them peeking in a window. So I just do what they say. It's easier that way. I feel better already, though. It's a terrible thing to say, isn't it? To be glad they caught you? I've been awfully lonely."

"Have they treated you all right?"

"All things considered, very well. The food has been awful, except once when they brought in a meal from a restaurant. The bed isn't much to sleep on, and there's only one blanket. And it gets cold sometimes, at night."

Webber turned his attention to the bed. It was an old-fashioned iron affair. There was a soiled mattress, and one soiled blanket. There was no other furniture in the room. "Not much luxury around this place," he said. "You wouldn't think the owner was a prosperous attorney. Did you know the cottage belongs to Mr. Wilcox?"

Her startled expression told him she didn't.

"The question is, how do we get out? Let's see—if this was one of those melodramatic movies, I'd hide by the door, and you would scream, and as they came running in I'd knock them out and overpower them."

She sighed. "It wouldn't work. They have us arranged so they can see our chairs before they come through the door. They're awfully efficient that way. There's always one of them in the cottage, and when they get tired watching me they close the door and bolt it. Then they have the windows nailed so we couldn't get out that way without breaking one, or making a lot of noise getting the nails loose. They have guards in the woods, and these two take turns going around the cottage. I suppose that's how they caught you."

"I suppose," he said.

"I've been worried about Valerie. Do you know what happened to her?"

Webber responded with a blank, "Valerie who?"

"Valerie Johnson. Ruth's sister. She was with me—I mean, we were captured together. They brought me here and took her somewhere else."

"How did it happen?"

"I was going to the police station, but I had to stop off at the post office. Valerie was driving by, and she stopped and offered me a ride. Then as soon as traffic thinned out a man straightened up in the back seat. I suppose he'd hidden there when she had the car parked. He held a gun on her, and made her drive out here. They left me here, and took her somewhere else."

"Does Valerie look anything like Betty Parnet?"

"Goodness, no! Valerie is taller, and has a better figure. She's very attractive. Of course her hair is about the same color as Betty's, and...."

"She'd get by all right, as long as the people she talked to had never seen Betty. Yes," he went on, as she looked at him wide-eyed, "I think I know, now, who applied for that life insurance policy."

"Valerie didn't," she whispered. "She wouldn't"

"Perhaps not." But he was certain she had. And the man in the back seat of Valerie's car was only part of the act. What did it prove? It was like all the other leads on the Betty Parnet murder. It went nowhere.

The rain came with a rush, large drops which thudded against the cottage roof and became a rumble of falling water. Rain blew through the one partly opened window, and Marilyn, sitting close to it, squirmed uncomfortably.

"We're getting wet," she called.

The blond gunman came into the room, examined the window, and went out for a hammer. He cracked the glass, but he got the window down. Then he nailed it down. He gave them no more than a cursory glance as he strode out.

"That one is called Blackie," Marilyn said. "They call the bald-headed one Egghead. I told him that if a blond man is called Blackie, a bald man should be called Harry. He didn't like it.

Webber smiled, and watched the rain flooding against the windowpane. He didn't care to mention the problem to Marilyn, but he was trying to figure out why she was still alive.

His own capture proved nothing—yet. Blackie and Egghead would naturally hold him until they received instructions. As for Marilyn, her kidnapping had been carefully planned. Someone felt he had to have her out of the way, and she had been a prisoner from Wednesday until Saturday. She probably knew more now than she had when she was captured.

She could bring police attention to Valerie Johnson, and with the aid of a photo they could easily establish if Johnson had applied for the insurance. Marilyn had probably seen several members of the gang, and could identify them. Morton, whom she could have identified, and whose name she thought she knew was dead. She could do him no harm. But she certainly was more dangerous to the gang on Saturday than she had been on Wednesday.

A gang which had already committed three murders, Webber thought, would not become squeamish at the prospect of a fourth. Why all the elaborate arrangements to look after Marilyn Andrews? Guards in the cottage, guards in the woods—at best she was a nuisance to them. They did not dare have her escape. The man called Egghead had said she was to be killed if there was any rescue attempt. Killing her would clearly save them both trouble and risk. So why was she alive?

He said to Marilyn, "The basis for all this mess is still that insurance application. Can you think of any reason Valerie Johnson would want to use Betty Parnet's name for something like that?"

She shook her head. "None of us know Valerie very well. I saw her a few times at Ruth's place—that's all. I don't know where she lives, or even where she works."

"Is she married?"

"I don't think so. I don't think she ever wears a wedding ring."

"Did you know Ruth has disappeared?"

She didn't, and he told her about that, and about the insurance policy Ruth had applied for.

"I don't believe it," she said. "Ruth was never in a hurry to spend money, and when Betty and I were thinking about buying small insurance policies, she told us insurance wasn't a good investment."

"Would she have nearly nineteen hundred dollars to pay for insurance?"

"She might have had that much money. She was awfully thrifty. Some of the girls called her tight."

"So she could have paid it once, but that was an annual premium. She would have to pay it every year, which would be rough even for a switchboard-receptionist. Well—the police might be able to fit these things in somewhere."

She said soberly, "I've been afraid the police would find out where I was. They would try to rescue me, and I'd be dead before they got here. All the guards have told me that, and I'm sure they meant it. And then last night—" She shivered. "—Last night there was some shooting off in the woods, and Egghead came in with his gun. He was ready to shoot me, if anyone came near here. I suppose it's a cowardly way to think about it, but I've been hoping that I could sit here until all this trouble goes away."

"Trouble like this doesn't go away. It just gets worse."

He was beginning to worry about the note he'd left for Sheriff Murphy. He'd made the situation plain enough, but one never knew how a law-enforcement officer would react. He thought maybe he'd goofed properly on that one.

They sat listening to the rain. One of the guards had ventured out into it, and they heard him stomping about in the next room, swearing bitterly. It was Blackie, and when he appeared in the doorway a moment later, the water had plastered down his fluffy blond hair.

"Game Warden," he said to Webber, "what's the penalty for fishing without a license?"

"You don't look like the outdoor type."

"I've been sitting here looking at that water long enough to grow fins. They say the fish are big in this lake. What's the penalty?"

"Go ahead and fish, and don't worry about the consequences. The penalty for first-degree murder is death, and even if you're caught fishing without a license they won't execute you twice."

Blackie walked over and slapped Webber's face hard. But he did not seem angry.

After he had gone, Webber looked apprehensively at Marilyn. He expected a lecture on how best to conduct oneself when one is in the power of one's enemies. But she asked anxiously, "Did he hurt you?"

The rain diminished gradually. Webber began to wonder about the time. He had left his wristwatch in the car, because it had his name engraved on the back, and he regretted it.

Marilyn said, "It really doesn't matter. The meals come right on schedule—such as they are."

A clock was ticking loudly in the next room. Webber's curiosity became irrepressible. "What time is it?" he called.

"You aren't going anywhere," Blackie replied.

They heard a car approaching the cottage. The door banged. "Maybe the relief force is early tonight," Marilyn said. "They change the guards every night. Usually it's late—about midnight, I guess. One day out here, and they have to go back to town and rest up. They have an apartment somewhere in town."

"They *had* an apartment," Webber said, grim at the thought of the news the car might be bringing. "And don't be surprised if the relief is late tonight."

He told her about the raid on the apartment, and she recognized the men he described. "Mike and Jack," she said. "I hope the jail cooking is as bad as theirs was."

Webber spoke softly. "Marilyn, we'll have to get out of here. Are you up to it?"

"I don't know. I thought about it myself, at first, but I didn't see any way. How would we do it?"

"We'll have to think of something. These men are killers.

The raid on their apartment, and my walking in here, might make them nervous. Do you see?"

"Yes. And I know at least six of them by sight. I've thought about that."

"So when they start getting nervous, it would be best if we weren't around." He didn't mention the note to Sheriff Murphy. There was no point in worrying her about that.

The car drove off. The door banged again, but no one came into the bedroom. Webber looked about disgustedly. The only available weapon seemed to be the chair he was sitting on. It was much too solid for his satisfaction. He doubted that he could dismantle it without making a noise.

In the next room, someone was going through the motions of cooking, using the gasoline stove. Webber's late lunch, and the blended aroma of food and gasoline fumes, did nothing to sharpen his appetite.

"Since they obviously can't cook," he said, "did you offer to cook for them?"

"No. I didn't want to be too friendly with them."

"It's a thought, though. There are a lot of angles we could work, if we had time." But not many that would work before ten o'clock.

Blackie brought in a plate of beans, and a cup of horribly black coffee. He stood in the doorway absently, gun in hand, and watched Marilyn eat. Webber said earnestly, "Gentlemen, I had a late lunch today, and I'm not hungry now. I'll probably be starved by midnight. Do you suppose…?"

"He don't like the looks of my cooking," Blackie said. "If I'd knew you were coming, Webber, I'd have made butterfly-brain fricassee, or something. That's what you get for dropping in unannounced."

From the next room, Egghead said, "We usually eat something later. We'll cut you in."

"Thanks," Webber said.

"If you're still here by then. You may not be. Blackie, escort the young lady to the bathroom."

"Sure," Blackie said. "Come along dearie."

The rain stopped completely, but the overcast sky brought an early dusk. Blackie and Egghead left the bedroom door open, and they hung a lantern on the wall in the other room, and engaged in a profane, table-thumping argument about a couple of race horses.

Webber whispered, "Can you hear me?"

Her nod was barely visible in the growing darkness. She whispered back, "Yes."

"What's in the bathroom? Anything we could use?"

"It's dirty. There are some rags piled in one corner, and an old brush of some kind. What could we use?"

"Isn't there anything else?"

"There's an old medicine cabinet. The door hangs on one hinge. Nothing important in it. No rat poison."

"Think, now," Webber said. "I want to know everything that's in it."

"I look at it every time I go in just to have something to do. There's an iodine bottle, contents dried up. A small bottle of aspirin tablets, half full. A couple of bottles with pills in them but no labels. A couple of old tooth brushes. A bottle of rubbing alcohol. Let's see. A box of band aids, and I don't know if there's anything in it. A roll of adhesive tape, or at least the metal thing that holds adhesive tape. I can't think of anything else. It isn't much for a prison break, is it?"

"Maybe not. Is there a water glass in the bathroom?"

"A dirty one. No sane person would use it. And there's one of these plastic tumblers, courtesy of our guards, I think."

"It isn't much," Webber said. It wasn't much, but it would have to be enough.

The darkness deepened. The clock in the next room ticked on loudly, and however Webber looked at the situation he knew that time was running out. These out-of-town crooks had stirred up an overdose of trouble for themselves, and whether or not they'd accomplished what they wanted to accomplish, whether or not Sheriff Murphy arrived on the scene, they'd be moving on. When they moved, they wouldn't want extra passengers.

Blackie and Egghead were playing poker. They whacked the table as they played their cards, and seemed to be generally enjoying themselves. Webber edged his chair out from the wall and rocked carefully back and forth on the two rear legs, thinking.

He had an idea, but making it work was quite another thing. He hadn't been able to make any sense out of the men's movements. When one of them left the cottage, he might be back in two minutes, or in fifteen. It would be nice to have only one man to cope with, but it wouldn't be nice to have a second opponent rushing in before he disposed of the first. Especially not where there were guns involved, and men who wouldn't hesitate to use them.

So perhaps he should make the attempt with both men present. At least he would know precisely what he was up against. And if it were foolhardy for an unarmed man to take on two armed men, it was less stupid than to sit there waiting to be shot. And he wouldn't involve Marilyn in it, so she would be no worse off than before, even if he failed.

He said softly, "Wish me luck."

Across the darkness, he heard her catch her breath. "What are you going to do?"

"I'm not certain. But wish me luck." He called out, "Ahoy!"

Blackie appeared in the doorway, and blinded Webber with a flashlight. "What's the matter?"

"Any charge for using the bathroom?"

"Be kind of rough on you if there was—you with no money. Come along."

As they went out, Blackie closed the bedroom door and bolted it. "Don't be all night about it," he said.

The lantern light reached the bathroom feebly, but Webber knew the darkness would be absolute when he closed the door. He stood by the open door and stalled for time. "How come the modern plumbing?" he asked.

Blackie had returned to his chair, but the gun still pointed at

Webber. "There's a tank on the roof," he said. "When it rains, the plumbing works. It's been raining, so you're in luck."

Webber closed the door. Plastic tumbler on the sink; glass on the floor in the far corner; medicine cabinet.... For the rest of it he would have to feel his way in the darkness. Cautiously.

The wind was rising outside. It came in unexpected gusts, and up around the roof something rattled when it struck. Webber carefully opened the door of the medicine cabinet, expecting an alarming squeak. It opened silently. His fingers moved haltingly from one item to another, and closed around the bottle of rubbing alcohol.

He had two vivid memories of rubbing alcohol. One concerned the maiden aunt who had come to live with them after his mother died. Every time she found a bottle of rubbing alcohol in the house, she threw it out. It was the drink of the devil, she said. The Old Man argued futilely that nobody could drink rubbing alcohol, that it was a good antiseptic and not bad for a massage. It was one of the few arguments he ever lost. Until the good aunt went to her just reward, there was no rubbing alcohol in the Webber household.

As for the other—he'd been fourteen, or maybe fifteen, and a mishap with his bicycle opened a cut in his forehead. The day he went in to have the stitches removed, the nurse saturated a piece of cotton with alcohol and dabbed it against his forehead. The liquid flooded down in his eye, and the memory of it still brought tears. He did not know how long the effect could be expected to last, or whether alcohol in both eyes would really produce temporary blindness.

It would be interesting to find out.

He flushed the toilet, and ran water in the sink while he knelt on the floor to pour alcohol into the tumbler and glass. The bottle was nearly full, so there was more than enough.

Blackie covered him with the gun as soon as he opened the door. He stared as Webber walked towards the table. "What's the big idea?"

"Water for the lady," Webber said.

"Two glasses?"

"One is for me later on. So I won't have to bother you again. Thoughtful of me, isn't it?"

Blackie grunted, and got to his feet. "You don't really want to drink that rain water, do you?"

"Rain water is purer than the stuff you get out of the ground."

"Not rain water out of that tank. I know for a fact there's a dead bird in there."

Webber grinned. "Are you sure it isn't a dead rabbit?" He was still ten feet from the table. He had to get closer, and he had to get Blackie's mind off the gun. "Who's winning?" he said.

"Let's go," Blackie said.

"How about letting me sit in. Poker is more fun three-handed, and I just happen to have the evening free."

"You're broke," Egghead said. "And we aren't playing for burned matches."

"My credit's pretty good in Carter City. I can give you a check if I lose. That probably won't be necessary because I'll be playing with your money after the first hand."

He took two steps towards the table, and then another. Egghead looked amused. Webber turned his attention to Blackie, and the gun, and took another step.

Blackie turned to Egghead. "What d'ya think?"

Webber brought his left hand up quickly. The liquid caught Blackie squarely in the face. He bellowed with rage and pain and brought his arm up to his eyes. Webber leaped to one side as the gun swung around. Taken by surprise, Egghead hesitated an instant too long. He started to shove his chair back, started to reach for his own gun, started to get to his feet, and the alcohol splashed into his face.

Webber rushed around the table, and shoved Egghead backwards. The chair toppled, and he crashed to the floor. Blackie swung in the direction of the noise. Webber ducked to one side, kicked him in the groin, and brought a fist down on his arm. He dove for the gun.

Egghead had his automatic out. He lay on his back, his

eyes clamped painfully shut, and held the weapon uncertainly. Blackie was doubled up with pain, and shouting profanity.

"Drop the gun," Webber ordered.

"Egghead dropped it. "Jesus, what'd you do?"

"Down on the floor. On your stomachs. Move! Do what you're told, and you might even get your eyes washed out."

He picked up Egghead's automatic, and backed towards the bedroom door. Marilyn was on her feet when he opened the door. He couldn't see her face in the dim room, but he heard her quick breathing.

"Bring the blanket," he said. "We'll have to cut it into strips, so we can tie them up."

She took the news so calmly he was almost disappointed. It was some minutes later, when they had Egghead and Blackie convincingly tied up, that she told him why she hadn't been surprised.

She had known all along that he would do it.

Webber had the presence of mind not to feel smug, or even elated. He was leaving in much better shape than he had arrived, and he had the girl.

But it was a long way out of the woods.

CHAPTER THIRTEEN

Webber picked up two heavy men's jackets, and helped Marilyn into one of them. It reached almost to her knees, and she laughed gleefully. "What a style!"

"Practical," Webber said. "We have a long walk through the woods, and we can't use the road. It won't be a picnic."

"It'll be a joy just to be walking."

He put on the other jacket, and tucked a gun into each pocket. Marilyn looped her arm through his, and they started out.

Pushing through the undergrowth had been tough in the daytime. It was torture in the darkness, but with silent sentinels lurking somewhere along the woods road, they had no choice. Webber took a good look at the meandering direction of the road, cursed the lack of stars or moon to give them direction, and led Marilyn forward.

The wind was blowing harder, and the agitated trees helped to cover the noise made by their stumbling progress. After a few steps Marilyn asked for his handkerchief, and tied it around her head. He could tell that she tired quickly from the unnatural walking, but she said nothing.

They went another hundred yards or so before they stopped for breath. They were already soaked from pushing their way past wet branches, and from the water shaken down from above. Webber's face felt raw from a couple of deep scratches. He had to keep looking ahead, searching for something, anything that would serve as a temporary landmark and keep them moving in a straight line—even if it were only a dim break in the woods a few steps ahead.

They moved on, shoulder to shoulder. He thought it might help if he walked ahead of her, but she told him no, and tightened her grip on his arm. He used his free hand to reach ahead of them, pushing the branches out of Marilyn's way, feeling their way around a tree. They stopped occasionally to listen, and heard nothing but the moaning wind.

He wistfully guessed that they had come half way, and hoped it was half way in the right direction. They stumbled into a fallen tree that lay directly across their path. He was helping Marilyn over it when her body went rigid, and she clutched his shoulder.

"Listen!"

The sound of an automobile motor was tossed at them by the wind, tossed, and snatched away, tossed again. Webber listened with a deep feeling of satisfaction. The car had to be travelling on the woods road, and it seemed to be approaching. That meant that their route had roughly paralleled the road. His worst fear had been that they would veer off at an angle, and walk for miles through the woods. He began to feel proud of his navigation.

The car rumbled closer, and suddenly seemed to swerve and come directly at them. They sank to their knees as the headlights flashed blindingly in their direction and passed by. When he helped Marilyn to her feet, she was trembling.

"Pretty good," he whispered. "We're only about ten feet from the road. We're doing fine."

"Shouldn't we get further away?"

"No. We'll try to go straight. The road just takes a loop to the north, there."

They started off again. The next time they paused, she whispered, "They'll be after us now, won't they? Maybe that was the relief men, and they'll find Blackie and Egghead."

He cursed himself for his foolish optimism, but he said cheerfully, "We have a good start. They don't know what direction we went, and if they come back in the car we'll hear them. I don't think they could find the Washington Monument in these woods tonight."

They stumbled out onto the county road with startling abrupt-
ness. One moment they were fighting branches, and the next
they were in the clear, with soggy gravel underfoot. Quickly he
drew her back into the woods.

"It'll be hard to find my car," he said. "We'll walk along the
edge of the road, and I'll have to keep checking. If you hear
anything, or see anything, duck into the woods. We haven't got
many friends around here tonight."

She sighed. "I hadn't thought about a car, but I'm glad you
brought one." She was very tired, and for yards she had been
limping painfully.

They turned south, with Webber making repeated forays
into the woods. He finally found the car by walking into it, and
banging his knee savagely. He was too delighted to feel the pain.
He found the keys, and unlocked the door.

"Don't slam the door," he cautioned. "I'll just push it shut. If
it doesn't catch...." There were more important things to worry
about than a rattling door.

She sat stiffly on the edge of the seat, and he tried in the dark
to get the key into the ignition lock. "Scared?" he asked.

"Just excited."

The key slid in. "Keep your fingers crossed."

The starter ground maddeningly. Webber swore under his
breath, and tried again. On the third attempt the motor caught.
He gunned it, and let the clutch out at the same time. The car
lurched forward, branches scraping viciously, and broke through
onto the road. He flipped on the lights, and stepped down hard
on the accelerator. She gripped his arm for support as he made
the turn.

"We made it!" he yelped.

But he held his breath until they had turned east on Heyers
Road. Or so it seemed. Then he stopped to slam both car doors.
"Next stop," he said, as he got the car underway, "a filling
station, run by a nice man named Bert Latham. I'm going to

call the police from there, and you can call your parents. And then we'll get you back to your apartment, if that's where you want to go."

She shivered. "It won't be the same without Betty. But there's nowhere else to go."

The thought worried him. The poor girl had been through a lot, and it didn't seem right to dump her into an empty apartment furnished mainly with memories of a murdered friend.

"I know," he said. "I have a wonderful landlady. Mrs. Mahoney. Her daughter got married last fall, and left her with an extra bedroom. She'll be glad to take you in. I'll call her from the station. No arguments. You can get a good rest, and decide tomorrow what you want to do."

He slipped his arm around her and pulled her close to him. She obediently dropped her head on his shoulder, and promptly went to sleep. It was a dreamy, exhilarating drive through the darkness for Webber, and he hated to take his arm away when they approached Ridge Road.

She sat up quickly. "Did I sleep long?"

"Not long. This is Ridge Road. The station is just around the corner."

At first glance Latham's Round Lake Service seemed busy. At second glance, Webber made out five cars from the sheriff's department, three state police cars, and two from the city police. He had completely forgotten the time, but the clock on the station said ten-thirty. Like the good investigator he was, Webber immediately deduced an explanation: Bert Latham had made the phone call.

They stormed down on him as he got out of the car, Sheriff Murphy, the Old Man, Hendricks, a blur of other faces, familiar and unfamiliar. Webber ignored them, and pushed his way to the other side to help Marilyn out. "Gentlemen," he said, "Miss Marilyn Andrews."

They made way for him as he led Marilyn towards the station. He got her inside, and as the Old Man and Murphy crowded around him, shouting questions, he snapped at them, "Later," and closed the door in their faces.

"Like to use the phone," he told Bert Latham.

The old man grinned at him. "That the girl? The one they were talking about in the paper?"

"That's the one."

"Pretty thing. I'd 'a rescued her myself, if I'd 'a knowed she was over there. Phone's in the corner. Here's some change— here. Have this one on me."

Marilyn made the call to her parents, and then she perched on a stool in the corner and smiled happily while Webber called Mrs. Mahoney. He told her about Marilyn.

"The poor dear," Mrs. Mahoney said. "You just send her along. I'll be waiting for her."

"It'll be a little while," Webber said.

"I'll have a hot bath waiting for her."

Webber hung up. "She'll have a hot bath waiting for you."

Marilyn sighed, and said fervently, "She doesn't need to fix me a bed. I'll spend the night in the tub."

Webber looked outside, where Sheriff Murphy was giving an exhibition on the efficiency of an elected law official. He was a super-charged dynamo, snapping orders and getting things organized. His booming voice carried in to them. "Get that portable radio out, and see if it works. There should be someone over there by now. Hell—we're putting road blocks up all over the place. There'll be somebody within range. Latham—hey, Bert! Come out here! How many men can go in the boats?"

Webber looked over, and found Marilyn smiling at him. "Your forehead wrinkles up when you're thinking," she said. "You look like an aged scholar probing for the ultimate mystery of life."

"That mystery's got nothing on this one," Webber said. "Did you hear what he said? They're going in boats. I didn't think it would work, because in the daytime, they'd be seen, and in the dark they won't be able to see anything. This wind will cover up any noise they make, though, and they might get away with it. Maybe we went to a lot of trouble for nothing. Maybe we'd have been rescued if we waited.

"I'd rather be waiting here."

"...Nineteen, then," Sheriff Murphy was saying, outside the door. "Webber! Come out here!"

"I don't think you'll have to wait here," Webber said. "Come on—let's see what we can arrange."

The Old Man stepped forward as they came out. Murphy deliberately turned his back. "You know the lie over there, Ron," he said. "Want to come?"

"I'd be glad to."

"Are you armed?"

Webber pulled out the guns he'd taken from Blackie and Egghead. "Sure. But we'd better save these for ballistics." He handed them over to Bob Hendricks.

"I'll find something for you," Murphy said. "I'd like to hear what happened over there, but there isn't time. You ride with me, and fill me in on the way." He turned to the Old Man. "I'll find some room for you and Hendricks, but only if you promise to keep your mouths shut."

The Old Man pulled Murphy to one side, and their argument sputtered briefly. Murphy jerked away. "Nonsense. Of course he did the right thing. It worked, didn't it? He brought out the girl, and he's the only one who knows what's going on over there. Let's get ready to roll."

Webber said to Hendricks, "Marilyn will need some transportation. A guard, too, until this thing is settled."

"Sure," Hendricks said. He ducked into the crowd, and returned with Pete Adams.

Webber introduced Pete gravely. "Sergeant Adams, Miss Andrews."

Pete beamed. "It sure is. Ronny, my boy, you hit the jackpot!"

"My landlady's going to look after her. You know the address?"

"I sure do."

"Deliver her to Webber's landlady, personally," Hendricks said. "And take as many men as you think you need to watch the house. If anything happens to her now, don't bother to tell me about it. Just drive off the nearest dock."

Pete led the way over to his car. The wind was still whipping viciously, but off in the west the sky was clearing. A few stars could be seen through a break in the clouds.

"Haven't you had enough excitement?" Marilyn said.

"Plenty. Too much."

"Then why are you going back?"

"I want to see what happens, and I have the idiotic idea that I might be able to help."

She said quietly, "There's more than that, isn't there?"

He smiled. "I'm involved in this in too many ways. Frank Milford was my best friend. I'd like to kick in the teeth of whoever it was that shot Mrs. Lamont. I'm wondering what happened to Ruth Johnson. I even feel that I knew Betty Parnet a little."

She gripped his hand. "I can't say more than—thank you."

With Pete Adams looking on benevolently, he leaned forward and kissed her. He helped her into the police car, and stood watching as it drove away.

Hendricks came up, and stood silently beside him. Webber said, "Do you think this will wind it up?"

"We probably won't find anything over there but the out-of-town element. I'm having Wilcox picked up in town."

"Do you think it was Wilcox?"

"I had a hunch it might be. He had the best motive."

"Motive? To kill Betty Parnet?"

"To get Howard in trouble. When you have murder along with an insurance policy, you always look first at the beneficiary. That's elementary. By having that application made in Betty Parnet's name, he automatically made Howard the number one suspect in the Parnet murder. Wilcox and Howard have been having a class A row. They've scrapped before, but never like this. Howard is threatening all that Wilcox holds near and dear. It adds up."

"How do Mrs. Lamont and Ruth Johnson fit into that?"

"I haven't the vaguest idea. If we pick up enough people, someone will talk."

"What about the two you got this afternoon?"

"They don't know anything about anything. They say."

Webber gripped his arm. "I almost forgot. I know who your mystery woman is. Valerie Johnson. Ruth Johnson's sister."

Hendricks said indifferently. "Do you think so?"

"What's come over you? On Tuesday you'd have given your eye teeth and toe nails to know who that woman was. Now you're not interested?"

"Oh, I'm interested. We've had a want out on Valerie Johnson since Thursday night. Since you told me Ruth Johnson has a sister. Valerie is a former employee of the Star Mutual Life office."

"Damn! And the Old Man walked on you for telling me too much."

Murphy came up, and thrust a gun at Webber. "Here's your hardware. Know which way to point it?"

The Old Man's voice drifted out of the shadows. "He's not *that* hopeless."

Webber left his car at the gas station, and rode with Sheriff Murphy. Bert Latham was in the front seat, a hunting cap perched on his grey head, talking excitedly. Webber shared the rear seat with two deputy sheriffs, who were quiet and business-like.

"We're going to Roy Sump's cottage," Latham said. "It's directly across from Jim Wilcox's place. My boy Tom is down there now, collecting boats."

The sheriff glanced back at Webber. "This Wilcox thing kind of gave me a jolt. I've known Jim for years, and I still can't believe it. Did you think it was Wilcox?

"I hadn't made any nominations," Webber said.

"Most of the people involved are connected with his office one way or another. Still—maybe we'll have things figured out by morning. Tell me what happened over there."

Webber told him, and kept it brief. "You son-of-a-gun," the

sheriff said.

State troopers had roadblocks on all of the crossroads. They turned north on a county road that paralleled the east side of the lake, and Bert Latham slowed the sheriff and leaned forward, squinting into the night for the turnoff to the Roy Sump cottage.

"There!" he said suddenly.

The sheriff made the turn, and switched to his parking lights. The cars following them did the same. They drove slowly along the woods road, and turned off all lights as they approached the cottage. Latham got out and led the way with a penlight, which he concealed carefully. They parked the cars, and filed noiselessly down to the dock.

Murphy did not waste time. He got on the portable radio and checked with his roadblocks and patrols. "We have the whole area surrounded," he said. "If they try to get out the other way, through the woods, the road patrols will get them, and if they get by the patrols we have every crossroad blocked. How does it look to you?"

"You might have to go into the woods and dig some of them out," Webber said. "It won't be fun."

"If we have to dig, we'll dig."

Murphy personally supervised the loading of the boats. He placed Webber in the stern of his own boat, and gave him Latham's penlight.

"Just be sure nobody on the west shore can see it," he said. "It'll give the others something to steer by."

The sheriff shoved off, and Bert Latham went to work on the oars.

The shore behind them had slipped into invisibility when Webber walked out onto the dock. Webber twisted around, shielding the penlight with his body as he flipped it on and off. The wind was uncomfortably cold over the lake, and the water was choppy. From behind came the muffled splashes of oars from the other boats.

After a time the sheriff whispered something, and Latham grumbled, "Think I can't row in a straight line?"

The steady swish and gurgle of the oars in the water marked off the passing seconds. Webber had always heard Echo Lake described as long and narrow. He had been concentrating on his captors that afternoon, and hadn't bothered to look at the lake. Now he wished that he had. "How wide is narrow?" he asked himself. Lake Michigan looked narrow on the map.

Latham stopped rowing. Webber peered ahead, and saw nothing. The boat lurched, and Sheriff Murphy went to work with a rope. Latham had hit the Wilcox dock squarely.

They climbed out. Webber handed the penlight to a deputy, and he stood by on the end of the dock guiding the other boats in. The men from the next boat moved off into the trees to surround the cottage.

Murphy called softly, "Webber?" and came over to him. "Is this the place?" he asked.

"I can't even see the house," Webber said.

"Let's you and I sneak up for a closer look. We can't do much more until the others get here."

They moved quietly along the edge of the woods, circling the cottage. The side windows were blacked out less effectively. Webber stared blankly at the dim outline of the house, and pulled at Murphy's jacket. They crept back to the dock.

"It's not the same cottage."

"Are you sure?"

"Positive."

"Latham!" the sheriff hissed. Latham was standing beside them. "We wanted the Wilcox cottage."

"That's it."

Webber said, "The place we want was painted white, with a lot of the paint peeled off. This cottage is some dark color, and it doesn't have a porch. The cottage we want had an open porch. It's smaller than this, too."

Hendricks had joined them. "You mean it wasn't the Wilcox cottage?" he demanded.

"It wasn't *this* cottage," Webber said.

"Maybe we jumped too soon," Hendricks said.

"You must have got lost coming in from the road," Latham told Webber. "You got one of the roads that branches off the Wilcox road. That there cottage you describe is the one north of this one. Maybe five hundred yards up the shore."

"Who owns that one?" Hendricks asked.

"City fellow. Kind of a snob. Name of Howard."

The only sound was the waves lapping at the dock. Suddenly Hendricks swore, and went looking for a radio.

"We'd better get back to the boats and get to that other cottage," Murphy said.

"Maybe not," Latham said. "Jim Wilcox, he ain't been down here this year. If someone's in this cottage, they don't belong here."

"Using both cottages, maybe," Murphy said. "Makes sense—they're close enough together. I'll send two boats to this Howard cottage, and the rest of us will take this one. If we can coordinate things...."

He whispered his orders. Hendricks stood nearby, talking softly on the radio to one of the state police cars. "Howard. That's right. William J. Howard. Tell them to pick him up and hold him. How would I know where he is?"

Murphy was synchronizing watches. "We'll give you twenty minutes. Keep the lid on until then."

Bert Latham hopped in to row the lead boat and they shoved off. Webber watched the cottage uneasily. If these people were as alert as he'd thought they were, it seemed that they must have noticed something, or heard something. Perhaps they felt secure about the lake, and were giving their attention to the woods.

Murphy started to post his men. Webber moved away, following the edge of the clearing. Someone caught up with him, and stalked soundlessly beside him. "Who is it?" Webber whispered, but without an answer he knew it was the Old Man. They moved together, reached the point where the road came out of woods and paused.

The Old Man gripped his arm, and they crouched, blending with the tree shadows. Someone was walking along the road, walking noisily and fast. He carried a flashlight, which now and then flashed random stabs into the darkness. One of the stabs picked out a car, parked by the cottage. He hurried up to the cottage, opened a door, and went in.

"Murphy should get some men around here," Webber said.

"He probably has," the Old Man whispered back.

They waited. The cottage door banged again, and steps came towards them. The flashlight flicked about idly. There were two men.

"What can we do now?" a voice asked.

A second voice swore hideously.

The Old Man touched Webber's shoulder. "Can't let them get by. You take the one on the left." Webber crouched alertly, and said nothing. The footsteps came nearer.

A racket arose suddenly from the front of the cottage. Murphy's twenty minutes were up, and he was taking the lid off. "Open up!" he shouted, kicking the door. "Police."

Lights searched the clearing, and one of them caught the two men. They broke into a run, and Webber and the Old Man rose up together and dove. Webber caught the man low, with a good tackle, and hung on. Blows rained on the top of his head, and as they rolled over a hand clutched at his throat. Then Murphy's men arrived and the struggle stopped suddenly.

Hendricks called from the house, "We've got both the Johnson girls."

Webber sat up, and brushed himself off. Someone was holding a flashlight on the face of the captive, and it was a face good for several installments of nightmares. It was ugly, and it was evil, and it was livid with frustration and hatred.

It was Ed Ronson.

CHAPTER FOURTEEN

Webber knew from the start that it had to be a nightmare.

He was lying on the shore of Echo Lake. His hands and feet were tied, and just over his head swung an enormous ham. He could smell it, he could taste it, but he couldn't reach it. Each time it swung past he snapped at it hungrily, and missed.

In the background, there were voices.

He opened his eyes. Over his head stretched the light green ceiling of his apartment, which Frank Milford had once threatened to enliven with purple stripes. Across the room, sitting by the kitchen door, was the Old Man. He sat with his back to Webber, and he was talking softly to someone in the kitchen. Appetite-tormenting aromas wafted through the apartment, that of baked ham among them.

Webber sat up on his sofa bed, and stretched. The Old Man said, over his shoulder, "It's about time."

"What time?" Webber said.

"Too much time. The girl wouldn't let me dump you out. Spoiling you already."

Marilyn Andrews looked out of the kitchen. "Good morning!"

Webber blinked, and rubbed his eyes. "Is it still morning? You look refreshed."

"I feel wonderful. Your father took me over for a change of clothes, and then we found a store open, and did some shopping.

Webber sniffed deeply. "Very effectively, too. I'll be with you presently."

It was the Old Man's way, he thought. Forgiving, he took it

for granted that he was forgiven. It just wouldn't occur to him that some further discussion of the matter might be necessary. It would be a little late to start reforming the Old Man now, and Webber doubted that he wanted him reformed. The more he thought about it, the more he thought the Old Man's way was best. There would be no fuss, no recriminations, and no bitter grudges. It would be as if nothing had happened between them, and that was the way Webber wanted it.

He shaved, treated himself to a fast shower, and went out to find Marilyn setting the table. "Who's on duty?" he said to his dad.

"On duty where?"

"Outside. Didn't you let Pete go home this morning? He was so darn tense when I came in he nearly shot me."

"I sent him home when I came. I figured I could handle anything that came up. And since we nabbed just about the whole gang, I doubt that Marilyn will be needing special attention. Especially since she'll be getting too much of it from you."

She blushed prettily. She was wearing a dark blue skirt and a light blue blouse, and her necklace was of large, pearl-like stones, blue tinted. She looked very well in blue. She looked wonderful in blue, and it had to be her favorite color. "Handy," Webber thought. "Easy to remember. Her favorite color is blue. If I happen to forget, I can always remind myself by looking at her eyes."

She brought the ham in from the kitchen, and the Old Man prodded it with a fork and waved a carving knife. "Perfect," he announced. "Sit down, Ron, and stop gaping."

Webber helped Marilyn with her chair, and took the one opposite. "Obviously we're celebrating," he said.

"Certainly," the Old Man said, deftly slicing the ham. "We're celebrating my solving the Parnet case and you're getting engaged to Marilyn. And as soon as we finish eating, we're all driving out to Hunterton to meet her folks."

Webber looked at Marilyn. She was holding her sides, and laughing soundlessly until the tears came.

"Isn't this a little sudden?" Webber said.

"It is not. I know what a damned fool you can be when you set your mind to it, and I'm not taking any chances about you letting this girl get away. I proposed to her for you this morning, while you were asleep."

"What did she say?"

"She said she'd rather you spoke for yourself. Just another way of saying yes. You can get married next month, when your vacation comes up."

Webber laid down his fork. "Now how do you know that?"

"I called Boyd this morning, and asked him. I also called Wilcox, and he says Marilyn can have her vacation at the same time. I'll get started now, remodeling the upstairs into an apartment for you. When your family gets too big for that, you can have the whole house. I'll move into that storage room over the garage."

"That house is big enough for any three families," Webber said.

"Nonsense. You two shrimps are going to have five boys, and all of them will be six feet four. In their stocking feet. If I don't get one police officer out of this family, I'll come out of retirement at ninety, and join the force again. Stop grinning."

"He's a dear," Marilyn murmured.

"I was grinning," Webber said, "about you saying you solved the Parnet case. You've got enough ham cut for the next two weeks. How about passing it?"

"I can be a damned fool too," the Old Man said. "And you know it."

Marilyn jumped up. "I almost forgot the baked potatoes!"

Webber and Marilyn ate, and looked at each other. The Old Man ate and talked. "Got a complete confession from Ronson," he said. "Got the whole gang, except for one man who got away in the woods. Murphy is out looking for him now. He won't get far."

"Go on," Webber said. "What was Ronson trying to do?"

"Make money. Or go on making money. Heard anything

lately about corruption in the city government?"

"I heard Howard was going to run for mayor on a reform ticket."

"He was. And is. He might even be the party candidate, now. Ronson and Wilcox have been city attorneys for quite a few years. Wilcox is as honest as they come. Ronson isn't. He formed a couple of his own companies to bid on city contracts, and because he drew up the specifications himself, he could throw in a lot of gimmicks that would make legitimate companies bid high. Then he'd perform a neat little sleight of hand that got the contract awarded to one of his own companies at a figure slightly under the lowest legitimate bid. Once he'd done that, he would draw up a contract minus the special gimmicks, which gave the job to his own company at what was really an exorbitant price. It was neat, and he handled it so smoothly that nobody even got suspicious. And he was getting rich fast.

"Then Howard retired from his engineering firm, and started looking around for things to amuse himself with. One of the things he found was city contracts. Howard is a sharp one. He's an old fogy, but he's also a darned good accountant and an expert engineer, and it didn't take him long to see that things weren't the way they should be. He went to the city government, and they threw him out. Nothing wrong, they said. They really believed it, and they thought he was deliberately trying to cause a scandal over nothing. Howard called in a few prominent citizens and showed them what he found, and they began to make plans to run him for mayor.

"Ronson found out about that, and got worried. He had a good thing, and he knew Howard would stop it in short order. He played on Wilcox's party loyalty to try to get Howard to withdraw. Howard wouldn't, and he and Wilcox had a squabble about that.

"Howard didn't publically announce his candidacy, because elections aren't until next spring and it would have been too soon. So Ronson cooked up a very neat scheme. He'd do a lot of dirty undercover work, and link Howard's name with a few juicy scandals, and wreck his political value before he even started to campaign for mayor.

"He needed some strong men to do his leg work, and somewhere he got in touch with Morton. Morton needed a place where he wasn't known to hide out, and he wasn't averse to making it a paid vacation. He and Ronson got together, and Morton arrived in Carter City with seven men. Ronson rented that apartment on Baker Street, but he wanted to keep them out of town as much as possible. Years ago, during one of their friendly spells, Wilcox and Howard put up those cottages on Echo Lake. They don't use them much anymore, and Ronson was friendly with both men, so he got permission to use the cottages, and moved in his crooks.

"He had some hot stuff lined up. He had an unwed mother—she's only fifteen—who was going to slap a paternity suit on Howard. He had a fellow who was going to sue his wife for divorce and name Howard as the principal reason, and the wife was going to admit it. He was going to try and make out that Howard had bribed an assessor to reduce his taxes. And a few more things like that. He couldn't prove any of them, but they would all make the headlines, and after a few headlines of that nature Howard wouldn't draw a vote for dogcatcher in this town, let alone mayor.

"Somewhere along the line Ronson got the idea of involving Howard in an insurance scandal, and fortunately for Howard and unfortunately for him, they started out with that one. Valerie Johnson, who has been his mistress for the last three years or so, used to work in the Star Mutual Life office, and with Betty Parnet and all her records available, it probably seemed like a cinch.

"As they worked it out, it wasn't a bad plan. Valerie Johnson picked Jones, who went to work for Star Mutual after she left the office. She used Betty Parnet's name and applied for the insurance. She got herself examined by the two doctors. Then almost as an afterthought they thought of the inspection report, and they wrecked a good plan by carrying it too far. Greenway is perpetually in a financial jam, and his name probably appears regularly on Credit Bureau reports of delinquent accounts. Ronson had access to those, and noticed where Greenway worked. So Valerie dropped in at the Star Mutual office to chat with an old friend, and filched an inspection requisition form. One of Morton's boys got ahold of Greenway, and offered him five hundred if he would be at the office when the requisition arrived and rush the report. Greenway has now confessed. He took the five hundred."

"Wow!" Webber said. "What did Boyd say?"

"He hasn't spoken yet. It's his problem. Of course Greenway really did nothing dishonest in his investigation. He thought some business deal was involved, and they were in a hurry to get a policy issued. And he needed the five hundred. Perhaps Boyd will be lenient with him."

"I hope so."

"Ronson had his plan going nicely. The insurance was applied for, Johnson had been examined, Greenway had finished his investigation—they thought. And then Frank Milford started on the same investigation. Ruth Johnson tipped them off when Milford went to the Ronson and Wilcox office. Johnson knew nothing about the scheme, but Milford arrived right after Greenway had been there, winding up *his* investigation, and she thought it was funny two investigators would show up back to back. She talked about it, and that jolted Ronson, and he put a tail on Milford.

"He went right ahead with his plan, though. One of Morton's boys stole Howard's car, and Morton had already arranged to sell it to Betty Parnet. He drove it over to Sunset Boulevard, parked down the street, and did a little effective work on the steering mechanism. Then he drove it into town to 974, and sold it to Betty. And she started out happily to try it out. It really was a bargain, you know, at what he charged her.

"Right there Ronson's scheme fell apart. He hadn't wanted murder. He hadn't even wanted Parnet to get hurt. He rather liked the girl, and he would have liked to have known her much better—he was that kind. Parnet was supposed to get involved in a minor traffic accident, maybe involving nobody but herself, get caught with a stolen car, and the ground would be laid for a good scandal. Who insured Howard's niece's life, and sold her a car that was rigged to kill her? Did Howard do it? It was his car, wasn't it? Didn't he stand to collect the insurance? It was a quaint enough situation to get talked about and written about, which was just what Ronson wanted."

"Just screwball enough to be effective," Webber said.

"Right. People take well to insurance scandals. Anyway, Ronson's luck failed. Parnet got around the first corner, and her next turn was Suicide Curve. And Ronson's luck ran out a second time, because Frank Milford was on his way back to Carter City, and he saw the accident and recognized Parnet.

"The men following Milford recognized Parnet, too, and realized what had happened. They're the kind that acts first and thinks later, if at all, and they figured Milford knew too much. He got back in his car before they could pull anything, but he played right into their hands by stopping to make a phone call, and they ran him down.

"Ronson must have had a restless night, that night. His neat little scandal had backfired and dumped two murders right into his lap. He didn't think the police would pay much attention to Parnet's minor traffic accident, but he knew they'd pay a lot of attention to two murders. Where he lost his head, though, was when you started another insurance investigation the next day. He had you followed from the Ronson and Wilcox office, and he thought you must be Sherlock Holmes incarnate, or something, because you talked to those people on Sunset Boulevard, and then you drove right across town and talked with Charlotte Lamont."

"Logical, since Betty Parnet had lived there."

"Ronson didn't think about that. What he did know only too well was that Ruth and Valerie Johnson once lived with Mrs. Lamont. That was at the time that Valerie became his mistress, and Mrs. Lamont kicked up a fuss and threw the Johnsons out.

She also told Ronson enough things to make a lasting impression on him. So he figured you'd put your finger on the fact that Valerie was the one who applied for the Parnet insurance, and he knew it wouldn't take forever to connect him with Valerie.

"Then Ruth Johnson came back from lunch, and innocently passed the word that you were talking with Marilyn about Morton. Morton was in Ronson's office. He went there often by the corridor entrance, so the office force only saw him the couple of times he approached Parnet about the car. Morton didn't want any more murders on his record than he could help, so he and Ronson threshed that out, and Ronson called Valerie and they kidnapped Marilyn. And Ronson, gone completely daffy, passed the word along to get rid of you, Ron, and Mrs. Lamont. He got some of his mental balance back when he found that they'd missed you, and he called his men off.

"That's about the extent of it. Ruth Johnson knew her sister was involved in some way, but she didn't know how. She's nuts about her sister. Raised her, I guess, and she'd do anything to protect her, or at least she would have. Ruth went along with it when Ronson had her apply for the insurance and she agreed to disappear for a while. That was just to add to the confusion, of course.

"But Ronson also wanted to know what the police were up to, and he told Ruth the best way to help her sister would be to get information from you. She was supposed to go to bed with you, if necessary. She isn't that kind, and the thought of it must have scared her to death, but she tried. When you turned thumbs down on that, Ronson thought she hadn't tried hard enough. He went over the next morning, after we called off our police guard, and beat her up for not being sufficiently seductive."

"Poor Ruth," Webber said

"Yeah. I think she's cured now. I think she got some perspective on that slimy sister of hers. Anyway her bruises didn't matter because Ronson had already decided to have her disappear. He moved her out to the Wilcox cottage, where Valerie was staying. Any other loose ends?"

"Who killed Morton?"

"Ronson arranged that. When we started circulating Morton's photo he decided things were getting too hot. Some of Morton's boys were a little tired of him, and Ronson offered them Morton's share if they'd eliminate him. He thought there was a slim chance we'd think we had the man we wanted, and ease up a little.

"We didn't ease up, though, and after we knocked off the apartment on Baker Street, Ronson called a special meeting, to decide what to do. The whole gang was going to blow town today—get out of the state. The Johnson girls were going to California, and make a fresh start."

"What were they going to do with Marilyn?"

"Take her along, for a while. Then Ronson was going to bring her back."

"Why? She'd be just as dangerous to them later on."

"Ronson wasn't worried about that. He was sure he could—persuade her. He was getting a little tired of Valerie Johnson, and anyway, Valerie was going to California. He needed a replacement. He fancied himself to be quite a ladies' man."

"So that's why the special treatment," Webber said.

"Special as long as he wasn't in danger. He wanted to introduce himself as the rescuing hero after things quieted down. They were to handle her carefully, and kill her at the first sign of trouble."

"The skunk!"

"I could give you some better names for him. But never mind—he'll get his. That's the last of the ham, Ron. I thought you said I cut too much."

"I underestimated the cook."

"Don't eat too much," Marilyn said. "There's cherry pie."

"I've already given my housekeeper notice," the Old Man said. "She goes on part time the day you two get back from your honeymoon, and no more cooking. Breakfast I can fix myself, and lunch I can eat up town, but supper I like a meal like this one. The way I see it, Howard's the one who comes out best.

He'll get some credit for discovering the contract scandals, and he'll probably get elected mayor. He might even get his bridge partner back."

Webber looked at Marilyn. "I'm the one who came out best."

"We," she said.

"Fine," the Old Man said. "Let's finish demolishing the food, so we can start for Hunterton."

Webber shook his head. "I think we need to stop off at the hospital. There's a man there with five bullets in him, and a bandage on his head where the sixth bounced off, and if he hadn't risked his life to find out where Ronson's gang was hiding out, the gang would be out of the state right now, and so would Marilyn. We owe him our thanks."

The Old Man grunted. "Today I think I could even thank Pronk."

"I didn't know," Marilyn said. "No one said a thing about that. We'll have to stop and see him. Could we take him something?"

"Everything," the Old Man said. "Flowers, candy, books, magazines, cigars. We'll take him a truck load."

"I had something special in mind," Webber said. He got up and walked over to Frank Milford's desk. The little angel seemed to have lost its radiance. Jealous of Marilyn, Webber thought. Unhappy because there is another angel in the house. He had a feeling that Marilyn would be all the angel he would ever need.

"Sure, Ron. Let the Scarecrow have him. One week, and they'll be scrapping to see who wears the halo in the family."

Webber carried the pipe back to the table. "What a darling angel," Marilyn exclaimed. But as she looked at it carefully, her expression became puzzled. "Or is it an imp?"

"Both," Webber said. "It was Frank's pipe. I think Mr. Pronk should have it. It matches his personality."

"He must be a dear. Does he smoke a pipe?"

Webber dropped the pipe into a pocket. "He won't smoke this one," he said.

ABOUT THE AUTHOR

LLOYD BIGGLE, JR., science fiction and mystery author and musicologist, was born in Waterloo, Iowa in 1923. Relocating to Michigan, he received degrees from Wayne State University and the University of Michigan. With the publication of his first novel, *All the Colors of Darkness*, he became a full-time author, a profession he continued until his death in 2002.

Biggle introduced aesthetics into science fiction, utilizing his musical background and his interest in artistic themes. His mystery stories include the Grandfather Rastin and Lady Sarah Varnley short stories, two Sherlock Holmes novels, and the J. Pletcher/Raina Lambert series.

He was the founding Secretary Treasurer of Science Fiction Writers of America and served as Chairman of its trustees for many years. Biggle also founded the Science Fiction Oral History Association to preserve a record of science fiction notables' speeches and interviews.

He died after a courageous twenty-year battle with leukemia and cancer.